KICK THAT S O B's ASS

TRIALS OF TAMINA

WRITTEN BY BRENDA ALLMAN-DOW

COPYRIGHT © BRENDA ALLMAN-DOW 2009

EDITED BY TYRONE "THE BRAIN" WILSON 2014

BROOKLYN, NEW YORK

"A STRIPPED BOOK"

ADNERB PUBLISHING COMPANY

This is a work of fiction. Names, characters, places and incidents are either the product of the author's imagination or are fictitious. Any resemblance to actual persons living or dead, locales or incidents are entirely coincidental.

Brenda Allman-Dow

The youngest of three children was born in Georgetown, the capital city of Guyana. There she completed her formal education and later in Secretarial Science, becoming an accomplished secretary.

With her love for the Performing Arts Brenda proceeded on a singing career, making appearances in her native Guyana with the much noted artists of the day Johnny Raff, Tony Ricardo and others. She sang with leading bands of that era such as Bumble and the Bees, Mona Per maul and the Playboys and others. Overseas she appeared at the popular haunts of touring entertainers in Paramaribo and Nikerie Surname with many of their local bands and entertainers.

Later Brenda joined the Guyana Police, where apart from traffic policing, her secretarial skills gave her more horizon and she served in that capacity to many senior officers.

Her singing paid off as a member of the Police Women's Voice Choir and the festival winning Police Mixed Voice Choir. She even had the privilege of singing duet with the country's leading soprano Mrs. Evelyn John and on one occasion with the late Governor-General Sir David Rose.
The most memorable of her duets was with Ben E King when he toured Guyana in her early performing years. Brenda remained a member of both Police Choirs until she migrated to the United States.

Here she worked at many jobs, but the call of the lights was overpowering. Brenda enhanced her performing skills attending Little Theater School where her acting skills were honed. Following this she made appearances around the New York area the last of which was at Pearl's Place in New York City. Due to family demands, she chose to work from behind the scene resorting to her childhood hobby writing short stories and songs.

Brenda's first published work is the award winning play "Marriage of Convenience" which was staged both in New York City and Georgetown, Guyana to great success.   She has not put down her tools but penned two other plays "Suffering in Silence" and "Through the eyes of an Abused Male," Then two books "Innocent Lies" and "She speaks from the Grave." Currently she is working on other manuscripts which will be produced in the near future.

Acknowledgements

This book is dedicated to all the young women who have survived adversity to achieve greatness …..!

To my family and friends who labored relentlessly to assist in the completion of this tome. They boldly tract down all the relevant information of the places and times discussed herein.

I am grateful for the love and support from all, they kept me going showing they believe in my craft.

To all I must say "THANK YOU!!!!"

Reviews

Relatable characters. Inspiring story of forgiveness.

We should all be this evolved.

Andia Wilkinson
Reading Enthusiast

Life surely has a funny way of poking, prodding and kicking our butts, it has its way of redefining the strength of humanity that is buried within us all, such is the strength of the main character in this novel … Tamina. From her challenging formative years to a successful twenty first Century woman, this character embodies life to its fullest.

Finally we have a character with whom we can all identify.

Jeff Ross
Lawyer (FRO)

Preface

Quite often through the centuries women have been relegated to suffer subserviently, except for the few who rose above and beyond the fray. Despite all the male dominance it took a simple woman to be the mother of Christ.

The twentieth century saw more break-through for women, who from circumstances which thought to be impossible and the desire to achieve out-of-reach, just mere fantasy, have broken the mythical glass ceiling of ambition to succeed. Such is the case for the main character Tamina, she is one of those women. She not only made the grade, but won the fight to prove herself a phenomenal woman.

Proof that when given the chance our girls and our women after suffering so much ignominy, can truly 'will' good not only into their actions and lives but also of those with whom they interact.

The true metaphor of a woman.

DEDICATION

To my husband Herby,

I dedicate this book, this work of art. You inspired me and lifted me up when I taught I would never finish this novel.

You restored faith in me pushing on when the days seem short and my physical capabilities were diminished.

Thank you my love for always

BD

CONTENTS

Chapter I

Life in the Village

Tamina Sebe-Ankra lives with her parents in the village of Ngoziville, a fairly large and thriving community on the East Bank of the Beluma River, which provides them all of their aquatic needs, resources and much more.

Ngoziville has a population of about ten thousand with five schools and three hospitals all strategically positioned to provide optimum services to the community. There is a police presence though small in this district, some thirty-five personnel to cover the more than fifteen square miles on three shifts. The police though inadequately supplied and equipped have a 4 x 4 truck which is over worked and often breaks down. Everyone on the staff has an adequate degree of skills in repairing it from time to time. More often than not it sees more down time than necessary, because spare parts are not always readily available.

The station is commanded by acting Assistant Superintendent named Albert Chidi. His deputy is Corporal Roger Nelson, who was promised a promotion to Sergeant. Chidi is not a bright man, but has excellent deductive abilities and could reconstruct a crime scene better than the higher ranking officers and foreign trained personnel, for which he prides himself. His academic skills are not in step with his investigative skills and very often he relies on his Corporal to pen his correspondence which he would sign without reading, so most of his notes and minutes went unanswered, especially the requisitions for a new truck.

Six years have pass since he was posted here and no personnel have been transferred to or from his command, nor were there any promotions made. For this he is peeved and often burdens Nelson, who is a good listener, with his complaints about his Division being neglected.

Month's end is a joyous time as salaries arrive in the ambulance for all government employees in the district along with the much needed supplies for their offices and hospitals. Between salaries Chidi would usually accept anything from the villagers and sometimes share with Nelson. The other officers often get their perks while on patrol or by being traveling magistrates on their own accord, (which is very lucrative.) Known criminals are there main target, for they prefer to lose a few Nairas than their freedom and the constables are the welcome recipients.

There are neither street lights nor paved roads in Ngoziville. Animals are seen wandering about at will in every place. Sometimes when they wander in the market place vendors have to chase them away to protect their produce especially from the goats that eat anything in sight.

Oh what a mess when it rains, mostly during the monsoon season which lasts about two to three months. Known roadways are inundated by large pools of water causing people to find alternative means of getting around. The other hardships which occur have forced villagers to adjust their living habits as well. The village follows its traditional customs where the people collect water in large drums and clay containers at rainfall, store water in large urns in the huts for cooking and drinking where it remains cooler then fetching it by the bucket from the river for daily use. The use of river water during the wet season is very limited as most often it is very dirty and has to be boiled and strained before use. Modern conveniences are unheard of; the natives live quiet simple, but fruitful lives in the best way they know.

During the dry season outdoor cooking is common place, and it is interesting to note how this is accomplished in the rainy season, when there is almost not a single dry place. Some cook indoors at the risk of burning down their huts while others make a separate shed under which they cook. This suffices to a point except when it's very windy and extinguishes the fire. When this happens time and again it has to be re-lit, sometimes with wet wood as maintaining dry fuel could be rather challenging. However the circumstances they manage to get by.

This village is a farming community and many of the villagers work in their own fields growing various crops including plantains, yams, green vegetables, peas, beans and varieties of fruits. They also raise live-stock such as chickens, goats and cows. They reap enough for household use and many of them have a surplus which they sell day to day and on market days. Fish is a staple in their diet and dried fish in the rainy season is very tasty.

Saturdays are market days. This is the principal shopping day in the village which sees lots of activity and an array of foreign and domestic products and apparel, shoes, hats, electronics not to be left out the abundance of farm produce, as well as other items which are of lesser importance to shoppers. This is the day when the women especially step out arrayed not only to buy but to show off their dressy outfits. They take the opportunity to make sure they catch the attention of the opposite sex, to whom they sneakily pay avid attention. This is particularly evident when word gets around that someone has recently returned from overseas and is in the market place.

Most of these women are beautiful, varied in shades of complexion from the ivory with smooth clean skin and white spaced teeth in the upper front row of their mouths to the mulatto who could have passed for white. When they go by, whistles and cat calls are heard as their sway in provocative rhythm which attracts the attention of all, this is their natural expression, but some stride or strut to create wild excitement among the young men, some of whom express their desire of what they would do with this one or that one, much to the amusement of the others who agree and share in riotous laughter.

They all speak in their native tongues of the village as well as fluent English especially those who were abroad for some time and have returned home to live the simple life.

The other shopping days during the week are regarded as less important since only local products are sold and to a lesser degree bartered.

On market day the shanty restaurants do quite a brisk business with people from the far reaches of the village and beyond who support them for the tasty dishes and the convenience these facilities provide while they are in the commercial arena of the village. They still have good patronage during the week, but not as much as on market day.

After a hard day's work the men of the village gather at the local shop which also doubles as a bar where they consume large quantities of foreign beers, liquors and of course the local brew, palm wine. Having ice is not necessary but welcome when it's available. They seem to hold most things for the excitement of market day when nearly thousands of people, many of them visitors with their children from overseas come to get a taste of the real life and food, visit with grand-parents, in-laws and other relatives who are still resident in the village. The ice arrives by delivery truck with three hundred pound blocks which are delivered and stored. Sometimes half is lost to melting due to improper storage, so on market day what could be available is welcome.

The sight of motor vehicles is not uncommon though no one in Ngoziville owns one. They would come in to deliver merchandise from time to time, stay around for a while then depart to their home bases. Periodically they may stay overnight should they arrive too late to transact their business and leave before night fall as the roads are unlit and very unsafe at night. Bicycles are the foremost form of transportation but they are not sold in the village all the time, only by special order and would only be delivered when the trucks come in every other Thursday.

All the supplies which are not available in the Village Ration Store generally are replaced, the owner Chief Kalilah is very happy to be able to supply all the products that the local vendors cannot, they have to buy from him to supply their customers. Whatever happens they all enjoy good business and are happy.

Tamina attends St. Catherine Roman Catholic Secondary School the nearest to her home just under a half mile away. The children could be seen walking to school in large groups during the morning, on the broad dusty roadway which is unpaved but hardens during the dry season as much traffic traverses thereon. The Secondary School is on the same compound as the church and the Primary School is well on the other side of the fence. These facilities provide education to some two hundred children from age five to twelve in the Primary School and another one hundred and fifty at Secondary level to which they move on with the intention of preparing for University where most of them successfully progress with positive results.

Tamina, along with her best friends Stella and Mami, have higher aspirations of moving on to University after Secondary School to fulfill childhood desires of becoming professionals, though not clear in which discipline. Tamina knows she wants to help the less fortunate. This dream sends lights flashing in her mind and she is excited.

Children do not go home for lunch as the distances are too great for them to return to school in time for the afternoon session. Lunch time is only ninety minutes, so in the mornings when they go to school, everyone takes lunch in their bags and at that time they sit in small groups where they feel comfortable to dine, sometimes sharing or totally exchanging their lunches with friends.

Tamina and her friends Stella and Mami could always be seen together, Stella is tall and already a curvy teenager with long hair who always over dresses for the occasion with form fitting clothing of western design; speaks very little but when she does, chooses her words carefully to get her point across. Whereas Mami a bit shorter somewhat more full figured than the others with round features and long well-kept hair and her signature feature her dreamy eyes. She is the excited one who has difficulty expressing herself though when she is finished making her point it's valid but her effort is seems very laborious, more than necessary. Both of them are fairly well developed for their age and appear somewhat more mature than Tamina who is rather slim, with almond eyes a small pear shaped face a long neck, long flowing hair which she often wears up-tied and boosts a model's stature but wears clothing which does not expose her true physical attributes.

They live relatively close to each other about one hundred feet or so apart, Stella and Mami live closer while Tamina is further away. They often synchronize certain activities so that they can be together longer. One such plan is fetching water from the Beluma. Tamina lives nearest to the river although it is some distance away. Stella and Mami would have to go pass her home to get there.

Chapter II

The Trek

The distance from Tamina's house to the river is about a hundred yards. Traversing the level ground with colorful vegetation seen on both sides along the way. There's short grass immediately near the passage on both sides, taller grass and small trees a little distance farther away and these are overshadowed by huge trees like protectors with long boughs which sway majestically in the light breeze, shedding some leaves in the process.

The fallen leaves create a plush cushion beneath the trees where the lush under-growth provide secondary shade and screens which obscure the visibility of the clearings where lovers normally meet for privacy to express their stolen moments of passion away from prying eyes and the likely gossip which is sure to follow.

When the girls would leave Tamina's home they proceed along this path which declines as it gets closer to the river, then goes down some thirty feet of well-worn winding track. There branches on both sides to grab onto if needed. They make their way to the river bank where they're not alone but it appears that most of the women of the village are there, some sitting on the sand, some hanging onto branches, while others are either pacing aimlessly or sitting on their buckets which they've turn up-side-down intently participating in the conversation or just listening to juicy gossip.

There's a shallow cove in the river, a social meeting place where the village's older women would congregate to chit chat on current affairs.

In Ngoziville there is a lot to shout about, the younger women would linger there to carry on with girl talk, play games, whisper and laugh especially about the boys. Then they fetch water for their domestic use while the young men spend their time fishing and teasing the girls, making fun of them sometimes with acrimony much to their annoyance or embarrassment, much to the amusement of the lads.

Quite often a number of people are seen downstream swimming as it is deeper there and still protected by the reef which is part of a sand barge extending from the shore to about mid-stream.

On this fateful day with her two friends as usual, Tamina goes to the river, after their frolic and girl talk they're in high spirits heading home on the regular path. Unknown to them the unimaginable is about to happen, which will change their lives forever.

They sallied their way chatting and laughing, when they are suddenly set upon by a group of young men who were hiding in the bushes near the trail. There is surprise, fear and confusion, in a panic they momentarily freeze in their footsteps. Stella and Mami quickly recover from this episode that these devious youths are embarking on, but

Tamina is not so lucky. She is just standing there awe-struck, transfixed, opened eyed and scared, so they hastily turn their licentious attention to her.

She is cut off from her friends who are able to escape by running away leaving their buckets behind. The boys knock Tamina's bucket from her head drenching her with the contents in the process, roughing her up, knocking her around threatening her to silence, then dragging her into the bushes, lifting her some of the distance. Realizing her fate she fights ferociously, resisting, kicking, scratching and biting, desperately struggling as best she could to defend her chastity, but to no avail.

Her screams could not be heard, as they're suppressed by her attackers who stuff a small towel into her mouth partially suffocating her. Then while two of them forcefully hold her down, they take turns raping her over and over and over again to their full satisfaction; after which they run away vaunting themselves of their prowess and how they outdid each other, leaving her hurt, bleeding, traumatized, trembling with fear and wailing. Her injuries are far beyond the pain she is feeling. The scars, the insults, the disrespect, the abject depravity of these miscreants have profoundly wounded her so deep psychologically that her anguish seems even more profound.

Sometime later Tamina feeling well enough from her ordeal, tries to get up, a very painful process still crying at every step she takes, is limping and stumbling her way home. Her mother who is in the compound washing clothes sees her coming through the gate with unsteady steps and bawling runs to meet her and inquires *" Gal what happen, ah why yo a cry? "* Tamina tells her mother in halting and painful expression what had occurred and how Stella and Mami ran away leaving her alone.

Her mother Cynthia immediately faints falling to the ground. When she recovers, Tamina, her younger brother Reggie and baby sister Cleo are crying over their mother's propped up head, trying to console her. By this time a few good neighbors, women of motherly age are gathered and they help her into the house where they give her a glass of water. However she requests palm wine something she hopes would numb her wounded heart and calm her nerves.

Several hours later Donald, Tamina's father arrive after spending the day tending his fields only to be confronted with the very tragic news of his daughter's untimely deflowering. Angry and disgusted he heads out to the market place to have his fill of palm wine drowning his soul in an attempt to squelch his rage. *Those boys are trying the wrong person, I would kill them if I put my hands on them.....Kill them!"* Donald voicing his anger and pounding his fist on the table.

Days turn into weeks, Tamina descends into a sad and depressive state. Her friends come by daily to visit her but she refuses to see them telling her family to send them away giving a variety of excuses. Her physical wounds have healed but the physiological effects still exists. Tamina refuses to attend school and her parents didn't force the issue.

Resulting from the rape Tamina is impregnated and her parents are feeling totally embarrassed. As soon as her pregnancy begins to show, she is forbidden to leave the compound, however they're not sitting by idly. Since no one in Ngoziville knows of the rape, they were determined to keep it so. Her parents contact relatives in other villages with the intent of sending her to live with them until after she has the baby, but none is obliging. The last resort is her maternal Aunt Ruby and her husband, affectionately called Uncle Daan who lives in America. When contacted and told about the circumstances they are very happy to accept her since they have only one child. Ruby always loved Tamina, she feels that the closeness of living together would surely bond them.

All necessary arrangements are made for Tamina's trip to the US and her day is finally here, Tamina is leaving for America. Her mother, father, younger brother and sister accompany her to the airport a real trek for sure. This is the first time ever they have ventured this far outside Ngoziville.

They are flabbergasted at what they are seeing un-imaginarily tall structures of steel and glass along with traffic lights, paved roads and road signs. Policemen in uniforms with long white sleeves in some areas directing traffic and a large number of people hurriedly traversing the roadways, who seem to be going nowhere but in circles, occasionally the sound of car horns blaring or airplanes overhead distract their concentration from their immediate surroundings, as they gaze at them in awe.

They finally arrive at the Lagos International Airport from where she would depart on her trip to America. For them to see an airplane on the ground for the first time is a spellbinding event. Cleo and Reggie ask numerous questions especially one about the planes that made everyone laugh. They wanted to know how planes become so small when flying overhead. They seem somewhat perplexed and amazed.

Papa is awe struck seeing the airport shops with the merchandise they have on sale and the prices which are far lower than that of the village. Cynthia could not imagine that the wrap she is wearing is in the stores for only about half the price of hers. After taking in their fill of ambiance in the stores and restaurants, Cynthia turns to her daughter with a last minute word of advice, "My daughter, when you get to America with your aunt and uncle, you must be very good to them, they love you. Go to school and learn all you could and become a doctor, a lawyer or an engineer and keep praying, don't forget God is your strength and Savior."

"Yes Mama, I promise to do my best. I won't fail you."

It was papa's turn for his goodbye "God bless you and keep you safe my child. We will continue to pray for you every day and every night!" Cleo and Reggie hug her and crying spoke in unison "We will miss you sista, come back to us soon. Write us every day. We love you sista, we love you!"

Tamina is moved to tears, she tries to respond to everyone but words fail her. She hugs them all individually and then together and in tears whispering "I love you all!"

When the final boarding call is made, they walk her as far as they could with much hugs and kisses saying their good-byes again. Tamina walks through the boarding gate unto the plane and into her future to the "Land of Opportunity, The United States of America."

Chapter III

America

Tamina arrives in America after a long flight tired but excited with thoughts running wild in her mind, she tries to focus. "I'm finally going to meet Aunt Ruby and Uncle Daan after all I have only seen them in photographs and spoke to them on the phone." She can't imagine if she would recognize them at all. Having vague memories of what they look like and that troubles her. After panicking Tamina gratefully remembers some finite details about her aunt and the telephone number she was given in the event of an emergency.

Being a teenager under the age of 16, Tamina is placed in the custody of the air crew, after collecting her bags from the carousel she is escorted by a ground attendant to the Customs and Immigration area where her documents are verified, stamped and dated.

The agent looks at her and says with a smile "Welcome to These United States of America!!!!"

She emerges from the Immigration Screening and exits the doors to a huge crowd of people of all races and creed waiting for their love ones who have arrived from many other countries. Ruby spots her and shouts, "Tamina! Tamina! Over here, we are over here! Come around this way!" Pointing vigorously, directing her to follow the red lines on the floor to the exit. Ruby and Daan meet her and there is the repeat of that scene the greetings, quite similar to all that happened in Nigeria when she was leaving.

During the drive to her new home she has no time to really observe the awesome scenery as Aunt Ruby in her exuberance peppers Tamina with questions of the village and everyone she could remember, at the same time to a lesser degree telling her what there is in America. Finally with the very first moments to herself Tamina reflects on the day that was, kissing goodbye to the only family she has ever known, traveling from Lagos International in Nigeria to Heathrow International in England and finally onto Dulles International airport in Washington DC, meeting her long lost family who are welcoming her and opening the doors to her new life. With more fervor she wonders "How did Aunt Ruby recognize me? As far as I know she has no recent photographs. Maybe, my face is still the same but I've grown taller, I don't know but whatever it is, she knows me and for that I am very happy!"

Tamina's morning begins at 6:30 am way later than she is accustomed to back home in Ngoziville. She gets on her knees, talks to her God saying, "Father God, thank you for waking me up this morning I thank you for my mom, dad, brother and sister, but I especially thank you for my aunt Ruby, Uncle Daan and my cousin Iyke for giving me a second chance. It's most unfortunate what happened to me, but after I have my baby I am going to prove to everyone that I won't let what happened to me, keep me down, I'm going to make something of my life for me and my child. And Father God I am asking you to guide me in the right direction, Amen." She takes her shower, makes her bed and volleys her way to the kitchen where she finds another welcome party, the waiting staff and Aunt Ruby, who's drilling them on the preparation of a very special breakfast for her niece.

"Aunty…. It is alright I can make my own breakfast" Tamina says, laughing heartily Aunt Ruby responds

"My child there is no need for you to do so, this is your home now and they are the household staff. It's their responsibility to see to your needs." Aunt Ruby then introduces the staff Albert and Sheila to Tamina. She responds to the greeting, "Good morning, I am happy to meet you!" Then hugging her Aunt Ruby Tamina shows her appreciation and they both head for the dining room to have her first American breakfast and to finally meet her cousin Iyke who was all smiles and a shout of "Welcome to

America!" as he leans in to Tamina offering hugs and kisses. "Thank you!" she responds.

Iyke is her sixteen year old cousin a tall lanky American teenager with a handsome smile and a huge ego to match. "We're going to be best friends I just know it" Iyke expresses joyfully.

With a docile smile and a semi hug Tamina responds, "Thank you cousin Iyke."

"You are not going to corrupt my angelic niece" Uncle Daan says as they all laugh and sit down to their first meal together.

Chapter IV

Clinton, Maryland

During the weeks following her arrival Ruby takes Tamina around her new hometown the city of Clinton, to all the major department stores much to Tamina's delight. She is busy comparing what she sees to the Nigerian stores and sighs in disbelief as the prices are vastly different, so low and the products are much more beautiful and better.

With the task of shopping and preparing Tamina for the different experiences in the U.S. weather, Aunt Ruby goes about setting up appointments with the doctor to care for Tamina and her baby especially since her fourteen year old body would be under significant stress and hormonal changes.

After their numerous shopping trips to get her especially new maternity wardrobe the next stop is the doctor. Doctor Charles is the Fortune's family doctor, a man of great wisdom and years of experience who seems to move methodically in his practice. He very carefully examines and evaluates Tamina giving her a battery of tests, after being fully satisfied that she is in good health he issues certain instructions for her to follow. Aunt Ruby is keen to see she complies and makes sure she goes to every pre-natal visit as required.

As time progresses and Tamina's due date drawing closer there is excitement in the family. In the sixth month of her pregnancy Ruby and Daan accompany her for the much anticipated sonogram. This test will finally remove all fears from everyone's mind concerning the health of her unborn child and confirm the approximate due date of birth. Dr. Charles invite them into the examination room to which Uncle Daan declines. He then discusses with Ruby and Tamina the procedure and what they may see be it good or bad.

Doctor Charles is setting the stage for the sonogram which he will shortly start.

He applies the gel to Tamina's stomach and prepares the wand which he will use to look inside her womb displaying the contents on the system's monitor. They collectively held their breaths as the first images begin to appear for him to see, he looks up in a state of disbelief turning towards the family who now share in his utter astonishment and slowly speaking in a deep monotone, "I need you to relax as I must share something with you right now." Aunt Ruby answers "What's the matter Doc, is something wrong with the baby?" Tamina and Aunt Ruby begin crying immediately. Dr. Charles slowly turns the monitor in their direction and exclaims "You are having twins."

Tamina and Aunt Ruby begin screaming with joy forgetting themselves and where they are. Uncle Daan overhears the loud screaming and waling emanating from the examination room, could not restrain himself, he rushes pass the two RN's at the Nurses' Station and pushes the examination room door open, enters in only to find his wife and Tamina crying and hugging each other. Seeing Daan's facial expression of grave concern Dr. Charles decides to explain to him what is transpiring to which he responds with excessive joy and merriment, just short of screaming.

Several days later still in the celebratory mood of the great news, Ruby and Daan have Iyke and Tamina sit down to discuss her future and the plans for the babies. "Tamina you're only fourteen and a great life lies before you. We would like to raise the kids as our own giving them our last name "Fortune." When the children are old enough to talk they will call you sister Tamina and Iyke brother. Tamina you will go back to school to finish your education and when the children are much older and can better understand we will tell them the truth together. What do you think of that?" Seeing the logic and wisdom behind her Aunt and Uncle's statements they all agree.

Throughout her pregnancy Tamina's body is her worst enemy changing in ways she didn't know possible. First her legs swell to double their size. With her breast swollen and heavy causing some pain in her upper back while the enlarged stomach causes her severe lower back pains from which the only relief comes from staying off her feet. However the final two months of her pregnancy places her life in grave danger and that of her children at risk.

Getting ready for a family outing one Saturday morning Tamina had an unusually sharp pain across the lumbar region of her back after which she finds herself spotting. Scared, she yells for her aunt, "Aunt Ruby .... Aunt Ruby come quickly the babies, something is wrong with the babies ......?" Rushing to her side Aunt Ruby, Uncle Daan and Iyke find her crouching on the bathroom floor screaming. Iyke and Uncle Daan lift her up and rush her to the hospital for immediate attention. Aunt Ruby called this event a close call. Upon their arrival at the Emergency Room, Ruby asks for Dr. Charles whom she discovers is not on duty and another emergency physician who is available will attend to her.

"Hello Tamina I am Dr. Walker, I will be examining you today if that is it OK?", "Yes doctor."

"Relax ...... calm yourself down, now lie on your back and place your feet into the stirrups here. That's good you're a fine patient, now I am going to ...... examine you."

After the examination he reassures her, "You and both babies are just fine, but ....," and with that word Tamina begins crying as she fears 'but' always means bad news. Aunt Ruby holds her hand reassuringly in anticipation of the possible bad news.

Sensing their anxiety Doctor Walker continues "Tamina, the body of a fourteen year old is not fully developed for this task and the strain of the twins on your pelvis is actually causing some abnormal pressure. I am therefore placing you on immediate bed rest for the remainder of your pregnancy. No need for alarm, just a precaution."

Aunt Ruby gasps at the doctor's directive but tries to hide her concern as to not worry Tamina, "Yes Doctor she **will** remain in bed with her feet up like a queen" she said jokingly.

Seeing their concern Dr. Walker reassures them all again taking Ruby, Daan and Iyke aside to give them other advice Tamina would need to follow from then on to sustain her health and for her to have an uneventful delivery. "She'll be alright Doctor Walker we guarantee you that," Iyke said with much concern in his voice as is the whole family.

Two months later the family welcomes their precious twins a boy and a girl. Tamina makes it through the entire process relatively well and Doctor Charles gives all parties an excellent bill of health but reminds Tamina that her body will take some time to re-adjust and heal suggesting a further three months rest bit. Ruby then calls her sister Tamina's mother in Nigeria to give her the good news. Cynthia immediately announces to the rest of the family about Tamina. They hug, sing and pray that everything work out well for their American family and thank them for taking care of Tamina and her babies.

The Fortune family is pleased by the outcome and is so happy to have the twins at home. Finding themselves like kids in a candy store with the babies not even allowing the help to nurse the children even in the very early hours of the day. The assurance of Tamina's health given by Doctor Charles's report is evidence to Ruby and Daan that she is ready to begin her education.

Chapter V

The American Classroom

The day she long awaited is here, the beginning of the Fall Semester. Aunt Ruby accompanies Tamina on the first day of school. She is ecstatic and understandably apprehensive for her new experience, a new school, new friends and so many new opportunities. She says to Aunt Ruby, "How am I going to cope in this school? Everything is so strange to me. The school building is so large and so many children. Look at this, the hall is long and wide with so many offices on both sides with names on the doors."

The Principal's office is the largest at the end of the hall. His staff is busy in the front office while he is working hard in his inner office. As they make their way to the Principal's office, Tamina's eyes are darting everywhere like lasers in the dark, absorbing even the smallest details around her. Several classroom doors are open giving her the rare opportunity to notice desk and chairs to accommodate about twenty-five students and each room has two doors and many windows, back in Ngoziville she remembers a very small room with over thirty students per class and one door for the entire school to enter and exit. Here are green boards no black boards in the rooms she sees.

"Look how broad they are and a part slides all the way across the width of the board. It's really different from what I had at home. Will I be accepted by the other kids, will they consider me strange? I hope I can understand the teachers' accent and they understand mine!" Aunt Ruby places her hand on Tamina's shoulder and flashes a reassuring smile as to say........"Don't worry everything will be just fine." To which Tamina could only smile.

Her first interaction is with the principal a short bald fellow in his late forties with a bulging pot belly and an odor of cigars that fills the room with a pungent smell that lingers in the atmosphere. Aunt Ruby and Tamina sit with him for her school orientation, where he explains what is expected of all students. He proudly reiterates the facts of his school's ranking and of the alumni who have graduated from its halls to lead companies and nations. Ruby on hearing the praises lauded on the professional staff is more convinced Tamina's at the right place to begin her American education and she smiles contentedly.

However one sore spot came during Tamina's first week at school where she was teased for being different. Some students made fun of her accent this soon changed after the first class pop quiz where she scored one hundred per cent to top the class with her nearest rival some fifteen points behind.

From there on, everyone in the class wanted to be her friend and in her company, it seems their thinking that hanging out with her some of her smarts would rub off on them. She knows what's going on but plays dumb to their ignorance.

Tamina by her academic performance becomes very popular in the school district being known as that African girl with a brain and she is certainly proud of the moniker. She is guided carefully away from the troublesome crowd by Candace and a group of concerned students and teachers who befriend her while encouraging her to stay the course of her excellent academic performance. During times of sadness and great joy she always remembers the admonition of her mother at the Airport when she was leaving Nigeria, "My daughter remember to always pray, keep in mind you can be anything you want to be, when you get to America with your aunt and uncle you must be very good to them, they love you, don't forget God is your strength and Savior." She feels not only that compulsion, but also the desire of her own to succeed.

During this time, in her third year a small love interest develops with Terry the star basketball forward who wants much more than the occasional fleeting kiss she agreeably shares and her saying no to his amorous propositions, quickly releasing herself from his embraces, much to his frustration.

When Terry talks with his friends and teammates he usually boast of his girlfriend being the smartest in the school district, but angrily expresses his frustration of not being able to break down her defenses and promises to have that African monkey, then dump her. "She thinks that since she is so smart, but I'll show her she has no street sense, only book sense. She is no match for me. When I'm finish with her she'll wish she is back in Africa!"

After some nine months of their relationship Terry decides it's time to take it to the next level and to teach this African monkey a lesson, sharing this desire with his buddies.

Unknown to Terry among his group of buddies is Andre, Candace's cousin, who upon hearing what Terry's plan is tells his cousin. "When will this take place?" Candace asks. "He says next

Friday after the Basketball game!" Candace thanks Andre, than hurries to the hang-out and study group to inform the guys of the plan, deciding how to stop it without Tamina being aware. This hangout study group is a group of boys and girls including Tamina who regularly associate for academic excellence which they all attend.

Friday was all normal. The game is played as expected with their team winning and their supporters leaving the Sports Center in high spirits with much loud singing and conversation.

Candace, Tamina and three other boys, were walking together talking when their conversation was rudely interrupted as Terry Calls, "Tamina!" They all look around Tamina excuses herself and joins him. Terry then goes directly to the restroom area and into the men's restroom. Taking that time, Tamina goes to the ladies room. Candace and the boys pretend to leave, but instead go around the restrooms to watch Terry who didn't see them.

Terry leaves the men's restroom and enters the ladies restroom carrying a roll of duct tape.

Tamina is still in the stall, when two of the boys enter the ladies restroom behind Terry, he being unaware of them. The boys grab terry, dragging him out of the restroom and out to the lawn where they were joined by the others who are armed with baseball bats. They do not beat him, much to his relief, but threatens him like he'd never been threatened before. "You are to leave Tamina alone, never to talk to her again, never to look at her again. She's a fine lady, not your type." "I promise I'll do all you say!" "Now you are to make up a good story why you cannot be her boyfriend anymore." Furthermore for insurance, they force Terry to strip beyond his fig leaf then they photograph him in the nude, threatening him if he breaks his promise, the photo will appear in every ones locker as well as, the principal's office. Terry is now desperately pleading with them not to do so, as it would destroy his potential basketball career. "Well, all you have to do is what we ask you to." "I promise I have no other choice!"

They finally permit Terry to dress. He goes to the door of the ladies room to wait for Tamina, who has been utilizing that time before the mirrors. When she emerges from the room, Terry takes her aside to give her a story, says his goodbye and leaves her perplexed.

Within two weeks Terry transfers to another school. Tamina's friends never tell her what really happened or why.

With a massive work load from school, homework, friends and social activities Tamina carves enough time to attend martial arts classes a sport she's determine to learn. She remembers the pain suffered at the hands of the three masked rapist and vows no one will ever take advantage of her again, to never feel powerless as she felt back in Ngoziville. She discusses this with her aunt and uncle who understands her plight and enroll her into the local Martial Arts gym.

With her zeal and ambition through the years she climbs quickly through the ranks of the martial arts class from the very first rank of white belt to the rank of Black Belt. Her sensei is very impressed by her ability as he sees a great future for her in the art if she so desires.

She possess a strong driving force along with the loving care, advice and encouragement of her guardians propels her to achieve at even a higher level. She wants to satisfy that deep yearning to help others and the only medium that she could use was the medical profession. This desire is reinforced after her encounters with Doctor Charles. She sees him helping people and she wants to do the same, he has quickly become her role model. On many occasions of her regular check-ups Tamina would share her desire with him and seek his counsel on her future profession wondering if she would make the grade or possesses the will to stay the course.

After much soul searching as time is drawing near for applications to be sent out to colleges, Tamina makes her desire known to her guardians. As it's the case with all parents they sit in counsel to Tamina's future sharing all that is needed of her in such a male dominated field. Assured that she knows the time and effort that is required to reach her goal Daan and Ruby are ecstatically supportive while Iyke warns of the work load that is to come.

Unknown to Tamina, Daan and Ruby quickly call her parents back in Nigeria to share the news of her decision, after a few moments of silence a loud banging and singing is heard from the village on the phone, there is definite joy to the news received. This quickly turned to wailing as her mom speaks over the phone "My daughter did not fail me, she kept her promise and for this I am grateful." Still sobbing, she blubbers out "God bless you my child!" to which Ruby responds "Amen sista! Amen!!!"

Chapter VI

The Graduation

She did it! Clearly there is no surprise that Tamina emerges as the Valedictorian of her high school class and a recipient of numerous awards and scholarship to Columbia University in New York City to pursue studies in pre-medicine everyone is sure she is amply prepared for the trials ahead.

Iyke himself a junior at Georgetown University is pursuing a degree in Chemical Engineering with an added bonus of the rare internship at the leading firm Johnson & Murphy-Rose Inc., locking in the chemical engineering experience a field he long decided was his passion as it is his father's.

Daan works for the large multinational conglomerate "Johnson & Murphy-Rose Inc." where he's a Senior Vice President for the World Chemicals Division, a career which defines him as a true leader. The Fortune family is financially sound and will spare nothing to encourage and educate Tamina. She has solid role models all around her.

With Tamina's brilliance and intelligence she attends only the best schools, Columbia University College of Physicians and Surgeons is her next stop, a center from which many great people have changed the world. Tamina feels overwhelmed at the sights and notion of being there more so she feels homeless as it is the first time being so far away from her beloved aunty, uncle, Iyke and the twins. She calls twice a day and sometimes even more since her dorm room is so cold and uninviting not to mention the rude and destructive dorm mates who make clubbing a fixed class on the daily roster. Despite all this distraction Tamina glides through her classes completing credit after credit with the aim of graduating early with honors.

Certain classes are large with well-known individuals from the state and federal governments as well as international corporate executives are guest lecturers who engage each member in the student body pointing out to them the value of interactive participation; Tamina welcomes the challenge and becomes a visual figure of substance at each session. Before long this attracted the eyes of many both students and professors alike, it make them challenge her even more on every level, some argued through each session while others tried to capture her attention with quick whippets and small banter.

From the beginning of her first semester it became evident to her that living on campus will bring its challenges both in and out of the class room. One of her great feats came in the form of a young Irish-American named Raymond O'Donnell, a pre law student who always needs to win his arguments with everyone, professes to all that he always gets what he wants. A show boat in many ways but an honest and respectful character that seems to be always on his best behavior once

Tamina was anywhere close by or her name mentioned. His style is so direct that he intimidates all.

With her last year of college approaching she receives request of dinner and a movie from so many suitors, they keep coming and she spurns them all immediately except for that of the young Irishman whom she tells she will have to think about it. She remembers the first day of class with Ray being eventful to say the least. He boldly stood up and challenged their history professor on minute facts and won. She remembers him never backing down from any other challenges over the course of their three years in school. She coined the name for him *"the Irish Pit-bull."* It's with this bold and continuing courtship he literally breaks down her defenses after which she accepts his invitation for their first date. They are spending more evenings together sharing each other's company when they realize there is a mutual desire, they had fallen in love almost immediately without even realizing it.

From college to Medical and Law Schools their affection held true. Often studying the subjects they have in common together, they help each other with assignments and preps for exams. This concept garnered views from outside the disciplines to help formulate strong discussions with peers of their classes.

Chapter VII

The Proposal

Finals completed and their careers ahead of them, there is just one stage left in the evolution of their lives … "Graduation;" after the pomp and circumstance of the commencement ceremony Ray tells his family he will see them later since he's going to spend time with class mates whom he may never see again but heads to look for Tamina. Ray, Tamina and the Fortune family venture out for a celebratory dinner, during this occasion Ray takes the opportunity to seal his love for Tamina with a grand proposal of marriage.

As a gesture of his admiration and love Ray reaches into his left breast pocket pulls out a small jewelry box drops onto one knee and begins "Tamina Sebe-Ankra, from the moment I saw you in orientation class I knew my life will never be the same, from the day we shared our first fiery debate, you have bewitched my soul and from the first date you granted me, a date I knew I would move the world to make you my own. Today with all the love in my being and in front of your family whom I know means the world to you, I ask, will you marry me?"

Ruby, Daan, Iyke and the twins excited by this, promptly stood up. The excitement is toxic and makes all the others at the table jump to their feet with smiles and hugs except for Iyke's girlfriend Samantha. She feels hurt making her feelings known. She feels disgusted and angry, gets up from the table and runs towards the bathroom shedding a fountain of tears. Tamina and Aunt Ruby in disbelief follow her to extend some comfort but before they can say anything Samantha shouts, "Six years….!!!!! Six long years I have loved and shared my heart with that man and **not once** has he ever mentioned the words marriage much less engagement. I feel I have wasted all those years with him. I am such a fool...!" "Samantha this is neither the time nor the place for this discussion and it's one that you should truly have with Iyke at a different time. My dear calm yourself down he loves you very much," Ruby tries to reassure her. All three women begin crying as they share in her emotional state. Later feeling somewhat composed they return to the table to finish their dinner.

The family initially expresses their surprise especially since this is their first time meeting Ray in person although they've chatted with him on the telephone in many conversations; Even though they are so close to her, they feel that she should make her own decisions since she has proven herself to be a capable strong and competent woman.

Upon returning to the table Tamina looks at her "niece" and "nephew" then to her aunt and uncle who seem to project a vision of their trust in her to know what the best decision for her future is. "Yes Ray O'Donnell I do love you and I would be honored to be your wife." Kissing her passionately

Ray places the ring on her finger with a measure of contentment surrounding them all, Ruby and Daan bless and toast the happy couple.

Knowing that he has found his true life partner Ray's determine to share her with his family. Throughout his life his mother has made it her business to be-friend all of his prior love interests giving them her stamp of approval especially Katherine, whom she has long decided would be fit as the ideal wife for her son and mother to her grandchildren. Ray could not wait for her to meet Tamina hoping she would love her as she does him.

Days after the proposal to Tamina, Ray calls his parents telling them he has found the love of his life a beautiful woman and he is bringing her home to meet them on Saturday. Becky is very excited, however a bit disappointed it isn't Katherine but she is happy that her son has found someone whom he says is the love of his life.

This most anticipated Saturday came, Tamina is understandably nervous at meeting her prospective in-laws. She is going through the wrights of anticipation asking herself question upon question of what possibly to expect at this meeting, she never tells Ray of her inner most feelings as he is elated beyond measure of having her meet his people.

As Tamina enters the O'Donnell's home by the expression of Ray senior's face he is comfortable with her being a black woman; he likes what he sees a strong, beautiful and shapely specimen of womanhood. "Ray you have done well m' boy!" Patting him on the shoulder, but his mother is very upset and her facial expression couldn't betray it. Ray never told them Tamina is a black woman. She welcomes Tamina cordially then takes Ray into a back room and inquires, "What do you mean bringing a colored woman in our home as your girlfriend? What happened to Katherine, the girl with whom you grew up?" "Mom, since when does race matter, why is it an issue? That's not the way you brought me up. Everyone is equal in the sight of God, regardless of the color of their skin." "I am not being racist, it's just that Katherine is such a good and nice person, she comes from a good background, great family, she is going somewhere with her life. She is going to be a great lawyer just like you!" "Mom, do you know what Tamina is?"

"I know she is not a lawyer like Katherine, she speaks with an accent. Where is she from? Those people …." Ray stops her before she could say anything further.

"Those people, those people mom, I am disappointed in you. Let me tell you something about Tamina, you see that woman out there, she graduated in the top five per cent of her class, she is a Medical Doctor, she is smarter than I am so don't think because she is black she's stupid. You better treat her right, get used to her, because she is going to be your daughter-in-law!"

"My what, you guys have gone that far planning a life together?"

"Yes Mom and don't interfere. We will be having our engagement party in two weeks and three months later we will be married."

"Ray, what's the rush? You could wait a little longer!"

"No mom, I have made up my mind. Three months after the engagement and that's final. We can have the engagement party here or at Tamina's parents' home. What will it be?"

"Oh no son, please have it here. I would like to invite a few family members."

"Sure, but do not invite Katherine! We would like to keep it small with a few of our mutual friends and family."

Even at this point Ray does not confide in his parents that they are already engaged, leading them to believe that the function planned in two weeks is to be the official engagement. Just then Ray Senior walks into the room, "What's going on in here, how could you leave us so long Becky? Sara wants to know when to serve dinner!"

"Oh Pop, we just had something urgent to discuss, we are coming now." They re-enter the living room and apologizes to Tamina who graciously accepts.

Ray hugs and kisses her, much to the delight of his dad. Sara is asked to serve dinner which she does.

During the meal Sara is curiously looking at Tamina sitting at the table with those white folks having dinner, she is not the only one. Becky is sneakily observing Tamina to see if she is handling the cutlery in the correct order. Ray notices and kicks her feet under the table, which startles her causing the fork she was holding to clatter on the plate much to the amusement of all around the table. Becky in her embarrassment gives Ray a dirty look. Tamina feels the tension but says nothing to Ray and they finish the meal with quietness, no one seems excited but somewhat relieved that dinner is over. Then they retire to the sitting room to indulge in lively conversation as they see fit. Since Tamina wasn't totally comfortable of the reception she received on her first visit she decides not to return to the home again until the engagement party.

The engagement party went well and the wedding followed as planned. His mother did not invite too many friends and family to the affair as she was ashamed of her son marrying a black woman. Before the wedding Tamina and Ray purchase their first home in the city, a condo furnished with nick-knacks they held dear from their years at school along with the latest in technology. In the den there is a work bench, yes a king-size heart shaped water bed and lava lamps ideal for the young lover's experience. On their wedding night they went to their own home together for the first time with the promise to each other a delayed honeymoon after Tamina finishes her internship and residency.

Two weeks later Becky pays the newly-weds a surprise visit after ascertaining that Ray is at work and Tamina is home alone. The building security rings the O'Donnell's extension. "Hello Mrs. O'Donnell you have a guest here, she says she is your mother-in-law and would like to come up to see you."

"Oh thank you Jimmy, do send her up please."

She brings Katherine with her, Tamina has never met Katherine only saw photos of her but she had a good idea of what she looks like. Becky rang the door-bell and Tamina answering the door she is somewhat surprise to see her mother-in-law.

"Oh Mrs. O'Donnell what a surprise you know Ray is not at home but do please come in!"

She walks into their home and introduces the person with her as Pat. Tamina to the confounding of Becky says,

"Oh, Katherine, what happen, do you have two names Pat and Katherine? Do come in, we have never met, but I've heard so much about you. Please have a seat. Would you like something to drink?"

Katherine answers, "Sure, what do you have?"

"Go to the bar and help yourself and get my mother in-law something too, I think she needs it" with some sarcasm "I'll get you guys a snack, are you staying? Ray will be home shortly."

Becky did not respond, she is swooning in the surprise that Tamina knows who Katherine really is. She is caught in her own clandestine trap. Her visit is not a genuine one, she is hoping to create a situation where Ray would be so embarrassed of Tamina, proving her point that Katherine is the right woman for him.

Katherine gives her a drink and says to Becky, "Mom, Tamina is talking to you!"

"Oh, what did you say?"

"Tamina wants to know if we will stay until Ray gets home."

"Yes, I think we will stick around!"

After serving the drinks and a snack, they sit down to chat like old friends. Becky is not her true self and her face was extremely red.

Tamina observes her demeanor and sarcastically asks, "What's the matter mom ...., you look like a cat got your tongue?" During the conversation Katherine asks Tamina "What part of Africa are you from?"

"I was born in Nigeria, but grew up right here in America with my Aunt and Uncle."

"Well I must say congratulations to you and Ray. I hope you guys are very happy together. I must say that being a doctor has a lot to do with it."

"Thank you, there is a saying in my country, the blacker the berry, the sweeter the juice, I guess the berry won! Ha! Ha! Ha!"

Just then Ray walks in, surprised to see his mother he exclaimed "Mom! You didn't tell me you were coming and you brought Katherine with you too? What are you up to mom?"

"Ray my boy does a mother need an excuse to visit her only son?"

"Mom when it comes to my wife, **your** daughter-in-law we all know how you feel about her, not to mention that you also brought Katherine for your little charade."

Tamina interrupts, "Honey that's ok, mom can come over whenever she likes and with whomever she wants. It doesn't bother me, and I am finally glad to have met Katherine. Now I know she is no match for me. Then she gives her husband a solid kiss on the lips, she was not ashamed or embarrassed by their presence.

When Ray was released from Tamina's embrace he said, "Once you are comfortable with it then that's fine by me. So I see my wife is entertaining you ladies, let me get my glass and join you." With some friendly banter among themselves with cheerful laughter punctuating the conversation for about an hour mom and Katherine said their goodbyes and left in high spirits.

Chapter VIII

The Incident

Tamina and Ray attend a friend's birthday party, a sumptuous affair at an upscale venue where everyone is seated and served by roving waiters in an atmosphere so relaxed it is intoxicating. The music is soothing and compelling in the soft lights that set the stage for the next natural step for those who are caught under the spell of romance. Dancing is rarely passed up as even the lonely found a partner with whom to cut the rug, while others are eating, drinking and just having such a great time. The busiest area is the ladies' restroom, when Tamina sees no one standing outside that door she whispers to Ray her intentions and excuses herself to take advantage of the facility. Upon entering, her attention is drawn to the muffled sound she hears of someone crying and moaning emanating from a stall at the extreme end of the room. She listens attentively cautiously moving towards that direction entering the adjacent stall and climbing on the commode, looking over the wall she sees two young men attempting to rape a young woman. It brought back such vivid memories of what had happened to her. She became instantly furious and decides to go into action without even considering the possible consequences.

So infuriated, showing no regard for her safety, she rushes out of the stall opens the door of the other grabbing the first culprit tossing him out and delivering a drop kick with such force propelling him across the room; he ends up under the sinks bringing down the entire structure and knocking over the nearby garbage cans.

Over the sound of merriment and raucous conversations from the guests the loud crashing noise along with screams of help emanating from the female restroom, caught everyone's attention.

Without hesitation many rush to investigate the cause finding two women standing in the doorway in horror screaming since they are petrified at what's going on in the restroom.

A significant crowd of party goers were jostling each other to peer inside to view the commotion. The other scamp tried to escape but Tamina is too swift for him, she collars him and spins him around. By this time the first perpetrator from under the sink recovers enough to attack her from behind, bad news for him, she blocks his punch flips him in front of her then chopping and kicking them senseless grabbing both culprits by the collar and slamming their heads together. Looking down at the duo with scorn she says "Didn't your mothers tell you to respect women?" The crowd observing what is taking place, cheer and congratulate her for her bravery, among them is her husband who feels extremely proud of her for saving the young woman. She is now being ushered away and comforted by some of the female attendees of the function.

The spectators, especially the women are very energetic in restraining the offenders and really worked them over while the country club security came to remove them from the area to be turned over to the local police. One of the perpetrators in tears begins apologizing saying

"Man I'm sorry, it's Tim who says she's drunk and we should go after her."

Tamina reaches out and grabs him by his shirt collar saying "People like you give decent people like us a bad name. Now take them away before I have further cause to kick the crap out of them!"

Ray hugs Tamina and kisses her then asking "Honey where the hell did you learn to do that and how you never told me you knew martial arts?"

"You never asked and darling there are lots of things about me you don't know, but that was a long time ago before I met you. Hey a girl's gotta know how to defend herself!"

Life between Ray and Tamina deteriorates after that night, he seems to be intimidated by her, and he simply distrusts her. Since the night at the country club he feels that he knows nothing about his wife and her knowledge of martial arts, "Why is she so good at it?" She never sat down with him to explain her past. This led to their social life imploding never taking her out as before, since he didn't know how to respond to his friends if they should comment, make mention of her skills or even taunt him.

After three years of marriage they are divorced. Tamina now being a full fledge doctor is retained by the hospital where she did her residency, moves back with her relatives, leaving Ray in the condo. Ray's mother is a very happy woman particularly since they have no children. Despite the joy displayed by certain family members Ray senior shows some disappointment as he loved Tamina and recognizes the mistake of Ray junior divorcing her. He simply speaks under his breath, "Ray you'll be sorry, very sorry." With avid joy and unrestrained elation his mother in a quivering voice and trembling with emotion tells him, "Katherine is still waiting for you. Go to her. Hurry, she still loves you!"

Even though Ray is the one who initiated the divorce because of his pride he never really got over Tamina. He calls her ever so often to have lunch or dinner, sometimes she would go but would always say to herself, "Lunch and dinner is the most I'll do, I will never get back together with him. I think his mother and his friends control his life and I do not want to be with a man who cannot make his own decisions. When we met, fell in love and got married he wasn't like that. He has changed after that night at the party when I protected that unfortunate young woman."

During one of their lunch dates she mentions to Ray her intent to return to Nigeria and establish a medical clinic to help the less fortunate.
In a daze from the possibility of her leaving the country permanently but not wanting her to know this would destroy him he asks her softly "After your return to Nigeria can I still be friends with your family and check-in with them to see how you're

doing?" "Certainly Ray; they have always considered you family that still holds even after our divorce."

With their divorce final Ray walks around as though not in full control of himself he appears to be looking for something, sometimes talking to himself, consuming drinks beyond his two drink limit and most times curtailing his social life to which he has been a fixture until the recent past. When he visits his parents, Becky observes his condition and springs into action. She tells him to move back home so she can take care of him, but he will never gave up the condo they bought before their marriage.

The next course of action for Becky is to make sure he is getting enough rest and the right meals on time with loads of encouragement towards freeing his mind of Tamina. She forces him to take a leave of absence from his office to spend the required time for her to complete his therapy. Ray senior is highly annoyed that he pushed Tamina out of his life and out of the family pays little or no attention to his condition.

With progress evident Becky thought he is ready to be reintroduced to Katherine, maybe to meet and talk or even have dinner, she prays that their old flames would revive and nature takes its course. Despite all this he still thinks of Tamina and hopes that she would reconsider taking him back.

CHAPTER IX

BACK THEN

Twenty years earlier in the village the boys are making nuisances of themselves terrorizing the villagers and robbing them at will, the vendors at the market place and small boutiques were the main victims. Though known, they are never caught. Reports to the police are never handled immediately but the offended parties are told to take care of it themselves, since the police have more serious and important matters in their crime files to attend to.

Auntie Mabel one of the elder vendors in the market place has seen many changes come to her community some she embraces, while other trends simple fell by the waist side. She always considers herself a woman who can always find the good out of the bad but now these boys and their shenanigans have worn her down, she could not tolerate the criminal behavior anymore, and decides to take matters into her own hands to retaliate, possibly stopping them, the annoying harassment and the loss of cash and produce. She discusses her idea with some of the other vendors that she has a plan for halting the robberies and losses they are now suffering.

Carmen, the largest yam vendor says, "Auntie Mabel, whatever you can do to help us, we'll be grateful. We are with you one hundred and fifty per cent!" The others concur. Though Mabel did not spell out her plan, any possible form of relief is good enough for them.

Knowing that Saturday is market day with heavy crowds the boys would normally attack the day before when they know there is extra goods and cash around in preparation for the crowds on market day. Aunt Mabel goes home especially early that Thursday evening to prepare and arm herself with a bucket of stale urine and feces, all mixed up and rather smelly. The following day she brings her "gift" to the store, hiding it under the counter and waiting patiently to execute her plan. "Well boys, today is my day, I will give you the gift of your lives, something you will never forget. Ha, ha, ha, ha" She speaks to herself and flashes an evil grin.

The day starts as usual and business is brisk. The cash register is filling up nicely and the merchandise is disappearing from the shelves into the customers' bags much to Mabel's delight.

As the day winds down and the last customers begin to trickle into the market place when it suddenly happens, but this time it's no surprise, Mabel is amply prepared.

The gang walks into Mabel's store and begins doing what they do best. Ensuring that she is alone they went to work methodically locking the door from inside, filling their bags with groceries, then with gun in hand the leader giving Aunt Mabel a bag ordering her to fill it with cash from the register. This was about 500,000 naira. They each have three big bags of groceries and other merchandise. When the leader is satisfied they have all they can carry, he places the gun in his pocket and heads for the door signaling to his accomplices to follow him. They stop to unlock the door to make a smooth exit. With their backs turned to Mabel who is behind the counter, she seizes the opportunity to make her move. "Aha ah gat them now!" She whispers.

Being confident that this job is like other times, they did not pay further attention to Auntie Mabel. This gives her the time she needs, that little window of opportunity to execute her plan. She reaches under the counter, uncovers the bucket, lifts it while attracting their attention with a yell "Aay....." causing them to turn around with mouths agape and eyes wide open with precise aim drenches them all who are standing in close quarters with the contents of the bucket. It went everywhere on them in fact the leader yells out

"O' Gard some gone in ma' mouth!"

While the other boys are yelling "O' Shit!!! Shit Shit!!!! This woman throw shit pon we!"

Mabel jumping in joy says "Yo Bitch yo, Tek that, you disgusting pigs and don't ever come back. Next time it would be worse!"

They are wet, smelly and disoriented. Having no idea of what happened and in their confusion dropped all the bags, frantically pushing slipping and sliding all over each other to get out of the now open door and running through the market place, much to the amusement of the shoppers and other vendors who are cheering, laughing and voicing their opinions. "The next time you wouldn't get off so easily, you good for nothing thugs!" They were trying to outrun the obnoxious odor, but since it is on them the effort is futile.

Aunt Mabel picks up the bags as she begins to clean. She finds the money in one of the bags intact. Immediately she lifts it up and thanks the Lord. Some of the other vendors come to her store to assist with the clean up as they are very appreciative of what she has done. One vendor enquires "Aunt Mabel, what is that smell?" Shaking her head Mabel answers, "You don't want to know!"

From that day on the gang takes a hiatus, when they did restart their troublesome antics the marketplace was bypassed for other targets they thought to be more lucrative and less resistive.

Chief Collins one of the wealthiest businessmen in the country moved into the village recently. He bought a plot of land on which he built a beautiful house with fences around the compound making it secure. With Ngoziville growth, many have acquired vehicles for domestic and business use but Chief Collins is the only owner with a fleet of vehicles in the village. His fleet consists of two Mercedes Benz, one Black H2 Hummer and one 4x4 Jeep. For his leisure and security he employs three drivers, a gateman and a five member security detail. The house is fully staffed with cooks and maids.

Nobody knows the business in which Chief Collins is involved, but all that could be seen when the trucks arrive are large envelopes, a number of small boxes and crates addressed to him. Similar cargo is returned with the trucks when they leave his home. He lives well and supports the community.

From time to time this stately man walks around the village with his security, quite often stopping to kiss babies and give money to the young mothers and poor destitute people whom he encounters. No one knew his wife and children as they reside in the United States.

The individuals who raped Tamina perpetrated many more crimes, robbing the vendors at the market place, beauty salons and boutiques among others, but were never caught. They become bolder and that is their mistake. They break into Chief Collins' home to steal jewels and money they expect to find there. The rumor around the village is that Chief Collins has a business transaction which is worth millions of U. S. dollars and is keeping it at his home. But unfortunately for the crooks, The Chief got a tip of the intended robbery and moves the money to a safer place. When the crooks execute the burglary they find nothing. They are utterly confused.

When the burglars try to leave they find all the doors locked from the outside and the house in complete darkness as the electricity is intentionally turned off, feeling their way around they decide to climb out the nearest window onto a small ledge and work their way to a ladder at the end of the building where unknown to them the police are waiting in the shadows to make arrests.

They begin their descent and were about half way down, when the first going down feels his pants catch on a protruding nail and he couldn't free himself. Looking down he sees the policemen and tries to go back up pushing his two partners in crime upward until they become annoyed with him. He shouts to them, "The police are at the bottom of the ladder and my pants are stuck on a nail." They decide to go back up doing this, causes his pants to rip pulling it from his body exposing his bare butt since he had no underwear on.

They proceed up and another one of the thieves looking up sees three policemen at the window which they should have used to affect their escape. They became more confused and agitated causing the ladder to become unstable and fall. The policemen happily arrested them. They were taken to the Police Station, questioned and beaten with the hope of confessing to the other crimes which the authorities knew they committed but had no proof. These men endured all that was administered to them maintaining their silence not confessing to anything. They were each sent to prison for two years with hard labor for the burglary.

After the trio's prison terms ended they vowed never to go back. They now have evidence of what hard labor means permanently etched in their minds as a haunting memory which kept them in line and with that they decided to turn their lives around and went their separate ways to find their calling. They kept in touch for a while but as they went about with their lives connections slowly eroded. They're convicts, a title which will follow them for as long as they lived. They have to find a way to live with their new status and to live it down for all the right reasons.

Chapter X

The Dream Realized

Throughout her college years Tamina never stopped praying as her mother had warned her. Now at the end of this journey she is thankful and prays, "Well Father God, I did it, Thank you, Thank you Thank you even though you gave me two children, I think you were testing me but thanks again for giving me such a wonderful family who loves me so much and helped me to succeed. Amen."

By the time of Tamina's divorce and being a full fledge doctor she tells her Aunt and Uncle she would like to return to Nigeria sometime in the future to execute her desire of opening a clinic to help the less fortunate especially the women of her homeland.

Those who can afford will pay but who can't, will still be seen for free, no one will ever be turned away. Her desire is to give a service to her fellow man even if it would cost her. When she speaks of this as her childhood dream to help mankind, she develops a true brightness in her eyes and a certain peaceful angelic appearance which calmed all those around her.

Carl and Cindy still don't know Tamina is their mother and always address her as Sister Tamina. They love her so much and look forward to spending much time with her. When she told them she is going back to Nigeria they cried bitterly but Ruby and Daan promised them that one day they will go to visit her and stay for as long as they would like. They are consoled but waited anxiously for that day to arrive.

Two years after that conversation with her Aunt and Uncle, Tamina returns to Nigeria and is very happy to be home again since she left some twenty plus years ago, this is the first time she is touching Nigerian soil. She buys a beautiful home and moves her parents, brother, sister and their families from the village to live with her in a Lagos suburb.

The families are totally happy to leave the village for a brighter future and make no effort to hide their feelings from Tamina, who seems more grateful than them.

With part of her dreams realized she focuses her attention to complete her full ambition. She scouts several areas in and around Lagos that would be an ideal location for her clinic. Finally she settles her mind on one of the best pieces of real estate in the city which she purchases and converts to a modern day medial facility with state of the art equipment, not even found in the established hospitals in Lagos. While construction is in full swing she is head hunting for the best in the field of medicine, doctors and nurses who share her vision of helping anyone especially the least fortunate.

With everything complete she opens the clinic fully staffed, among the first hires are her sister Cleo who has become a State Registered Nurse and Certified Midwife, her brother Reggie a Sanitary Inspector and an orderly, three doctors, three registered nurses and office staff all efficient in their fields. This facility is up and running with clockwork efficiency much to Tamina's delight.

Four months after she opened the clinic a man came in with a pregnant woman clearly in labor. He speaks to the clerk at the admission desk, "My sister needs urgent help she is in labor! ..... Her name is Chioma." She is admitted while the man who brought her makes a phone call, after which four other people came to meet him at the center. He is anxiously pacing the hallway as Chioma delivers twins, a boy and a girl. The family is informed and there is high excitement especially by the grandmothers, who make sure they are there to get firsthand information and to be the first to see their grandchildren. They sing and dance then fall on their knees to thank God for the gifts of the grandchildren, but paid little to no attention to the children's mother. They briefly greet her. Her mother after some time had elapsed pays some attention to her wellbeing and had her promise to give her more grandchildren so she could enjoy them in her old age. Though Tamina had seen such displays before, there is something which seems different this time. She couldn't put her finger on it readily but she is taken by the level of celebration of the two elderly women. After she has completed her oversight of the delivery, satisfied that the twins are healthy and all the necessary duties taken care of, she retires to her office shuts the door to relax a little and reminisce about her own delivery and the last time she saw her children who still do not know her as their mother, but it is better this way for everyone, she comforts herself.

The children are now about thirty-two years old, Carl follows in her footsteps, becoming a Doctor and Cindy a Lawyer. Aunt Ruby keeps her up to date with the goings on in their lives, even though Carl and Cindy speak to her by phone quite often.

Interrupted by a knock at the door, snapping her back into this reality, "Come in!" she stutters. It is the man and some of the people whom he called, they enter the office and he speaks,

"Doc, my name is Kelvin Smith. My folks and I would like to thank you for what you have done for my sister. Her husband traveled and left us in charge of his family, so we are so grateful to you. We also took care of the bill."

"Mr. Smith you don't have to thank me, it's my job, this is the reason I'm here. I am glad you're happy everything went well and thanks for the payment."

"Thanks again Doc!" another voice exclaimed,

"But we must take our leave, so please excuse us!" "Thank you again!" They left her office with haste to tell the other family members the good news!"

Chioma's mother is so excited with her grand-children that she totally ignores going to thank the doctor for the safe delivery of the children.

Chapter XI

At The Clinic

The next day Tamina is in her office in the midst of paper work when there is a knock at the door, "Come in!" The door opens and Kelvin confidently steps into the office "Oh Mr. Smith how are you today? You are here to visit your sister I see. Is your wife with you today? I didn't see her yesterday."

"Thanks Doc, I don't have a wife."

"Oh come on Mr. Smith a handsome man like you do not have a wife!" "Don't get me wrong Doc, I had a wife but she passed away two years ago."

"Oh, I'm so sorry, but there must be someone special." She gorged for more details.

"Not really Doc, I haven't found the right one until now. I hope there is not a Mr. O'Donnell, and will you please call me Kelvin!"

"Sure Kelvin."

"What of Mr. O'Donnell? Tamina smiles,

"He is around somewhere in America." She answers nonchalantly with a wave of her hand.

"He is in America! What is he doing there?"

"He lives there."

"Where does he live in America?"

"Well, the last time I checked he was in Washington DC."

"Washington, do you mean you guys lived there?"

"Yes!" she replies, "I lived in Clinton, Maryland for a very long time."

"Well I lived in Washington for a very long time too, more than ten years. My wife was from there. Just imagine that, and we never ran in to each other." He sounds a bit disappointed Tamina laughed heartily, "What coincidence!" Then regrouping his demeanor, he decides to stretch the point.

"Do you think Mr. O'Donnell would mind if I take his wife to lunch?"
"Are you asking him or me out to lunch?"

"I'm just wondering, why he allowed such a beautiful woman to move back to Nigeria while he remains in America. Isn't he afraid that someone might just steal her away?"

"Mr. Smith, I beg your pardon, I am my own woman!" Strongly asserting herself her body language could not have been mistaken.

"No one can tell me what to do, nor control my life but God!" then a little more curt "Any how I can't do lunch today I have a lot to do, maybe some other time!" Trying to sound offended, but that did not deter Kelvin.

"Mrs. O'Donnell, I thought we were past Mr. Smith. Please call me Kelvin!"

"I am very sorry my intent was not to offend you," sounding somewhat apologetic.

"No, no!" With a motion with the hands," I like a woman who can stand up to any man. My late wife was like that, I admire that in a woman. I admire that in you! Anyhow since you can't do lunch today, what about tomorrow. If not lunch let's do dinner."

She is excited at the compliment, but tries desperately to maintain a straight face although she was falling to pieces inside. "Let me get back to you…. in a couple days, when you come to take your sister home I'll let you know." "That's good enough for me for now. Let me go see my sister."

Do you mind if I call you? I have your card with your number on it." Tamina laughs, she thought to herself, this man is determined. He just won't go away. "That's alright, you may Kelvin." Feeling better that he has made some head way into her armor he was lighthearted and left whistling Dixie. "Byeeee!" was the last thing he said to her as he was heading out the door. Then turning back opens the door and sticks his head in catching her by surprise, "Thanks for the compliment!"

"What compliment, I didn't say anything!"

"Yes you did, you said I'm a handsome man. Remember?" Tamina blushes, uncomfortably shuffling herself in her chair with an embarrassing grin which turned into a full bodied laugh said,

"Kelvin you are too much, very funny, you know how to make a person laugh! Ha! Ha! Ha! Ha! Now go so I can do my work! Ha! Ha! Ha! Kelvin quietly closes the door and leaves feeling more confident than he has been in recent times and says to himself "I got to have that woman, she's the kind of person I need in my life. I must have her!"

Tamina spend a long time in her office thinking about Kelvin. She says to herself "He looks like a very nice man, and I hope he is reliable and trustworthy. He makes me laugh, more than I can say for others." Her mind wonders back to that terrible day of her infamy, "All the time I've been back here I have never seen the violators, but if I see them I don't think I would recognize them since they all wore masks. For all I know he could have been one of them. Nahhhh ..., he seems quite a gentleman. Like I said to Pastor Luke, I have forgiven them a long time ago." Turning to the photographs on her desk she continues "I had two beautiful children who will never know that I am their mother for now, nor will they ever know their father, but I am satisfied just being their sister and in their lives. One of these days if I find the right man and get married again then I may have a couple of kids." A wistful smile creases her lips, looking at her watch she exclaims, "It's this late! It's time for me to go home." She promptly stops what she is doing, speaks to the night Doctor and leaves for home.

As usual Tamina's mother and sister attend the midweek Bible Class at their church and this Wednesday is no exception. Tamina spends the time to unwind and think in the solace of her home. She ponders more about Kelvin and his gestures until she falls asleep with him on her mind. It's the first time since her divorce any man has come this close to put her on a spot, making her laugh and enjoying it

Chapter XII

Their First Date

That Friday evening Tamina goes to dinner with Kelvin at the upscale International eatery called *"The Adnerbs"* a place where only a select few are allowed to dine on food grown solely for the purpose of *The Adnerbs* strong clientele.

Before dinner is served they enjoy a glass of wine, him the sweet red Chardonnay and for her the dry white Zinfandel, they are having small talk about America. Clinton, Maryland; Newport News and Busch Gardens, Virginia only to discover they were both in Busch Gardens at the same time.

Even if they had seen each other they would not recognize or recall any such chance meeting. After a good laugh they seem to have become more comfortable with each other and settle down. She compliments him for his fine attire; he seems to be a particularly well dressed individual, she likes that in a man. Then she goes on, "Well Kelvin, what do you do for a living?"

"I'm a Criminal Defense Attorney. I studied in America, got married to my school mate Clarissa Thomas. We were in a car accident where she was killed." Tamina gasps clutching her chest and saying, "Oh my God, I'm so sorry to hear that," almost in tears.

"I am lucky to have survived after being in a coma for several months. It took me a while to get over her, but after two years I have decided to go on with my life. Meeting you I know I have made the right decision.

"Mr. Smith you are quite bold, aren't you?" Tamina interjects, Kelvin sheepishly looks at her with a soft smile and continues "I am back in Nigeria especially to help people who cannot afford to hire a good Attorney because of money constraints either way they will have the best representation possible. It gives me a great deal of satisfaction giving to the less fortunate something I'm sure you can definitely relate too.

"Now, will you please tell me about yourself and Mr. O'Donnell?"

"Well you know my name is Tamina, I'm the owner **of "TAMINA'S HEALTH CARE CLINIC."** Mr. O'Donnell and I are divorced."

Kelvin is so excited that he couldn't restrain himself, he didn't realize that he is disturbing the other guests when he shouts "YES!" and pumping his fist. Tamina is a bit alarmed, she calmly asks "What is that all about?"

"Nothing, it's just that I like what I am hearing so far. I'm sorry, please continue."

"Well I moved back to Nigeria opened this Clinic to help people with little or no money too!"

"My dear great minds think alike. See how we are compatible? Now Miss Tamina, Will you marry me?" Tamina is startled but pleasantly surprised. She is laughing and choking on her drink

"Just like that, you don't even know me". "I know all I want to know about you."

"Slow down Mr. Smith!"

"My name is Kelvin, and why should I slow down? I saw you, I fell in love with you, love at first sight and I want to make you my wife!" "You don't even know if I am a serial killer or some closet criminal and on our first date you want to marry me?

Could we please change the subject? You're making me uncomfortable."

"Ok I will for now but you know I will never give up until you are my wife, to have and to hold forever!"

The evening continues with more wine and brisk conversations about current events of the day, likes and dislikes of each other. The rest of the evening is cordial, dinner is good, but Kelvin couldn't down-play his amusement at her embarrassment when she caught him cleverly eyeing her especially over the rim of his glass.

Sunday came, like the early days of her life it is family worship at the neighborhood church.

Tamina, her parents, siblings and their families go to first service as it affords them the rest of the day without break to spend anyway they see fit.

Kelvin and Tamina's courtship continue for several months. The comfort level is sincere and very often they act like kids with a new toy, embracing, bird feeding each other, giggling and chasing, then when one is caught, the reward is a kiss. They are absolutely happy with one another and the world. Ventures to the beach for private picnics and doing what lovers do as the mood strikes them but their playtime is reserved for Saturdays, when they can spend the whole day together. Then sometimes for a change they go driving in the country, stopping for a meal at a village open air restaurant where they could still enjoy a closer touch with ancestry and the wholesome atmosphere. They will also visit the parks and museums especially where they share common interests.

Many times Kelvin would observe Tamina in a blank stare as though in deep thought in a world of her own. One such occasion when they were at the Golden Rooster Restaurant dining on the balcony, he asks what is troubling her so much that she forgets he is even there,

"You seem lost in space. What happened?" She is thinking of what those hooligans did to her, but she never tells him. Tamina would only flash him a winsome smile pat him on the cheek then kiss him. "It's nothing honey. I'm just reflecting on my life and my good fortune to have met you!" To which the now exceptionally happy Kelvin would reply, "That better be!" He was really elated at this and shows it.

"K my darling" As she fondly calls him, with some melody in her voice and a coquettish smile, "Some months ago, on our first date you were pushing me into a corner. Remember?" She was aimlessly stirring her glass with the cocktail straw. "You asked me a certain question, do you remember? Will you ask me that question again, now?"

Without hesitation he broke into a huge smile, clapping his hands and falls on one knee, takes her left hand and says, "Tamina O'Donnell, would you please make me the happiest man in the world, will you marry me?" By this time the other patrons are looking on and those who are not so close drew nearer to get a first-hand view and witness the spectacle. "Oh yes, I would marry you, I would marry you and I **would** marry you only on one condition". He is now troubled, his face couldn't betray how he feels and the audience perplex. "What might that condition be?" He was hesitant not knowing what to expect. She gives him a mischievous grin, a wink of the eye and shouts, "That you don't ever change from what you are doing now. I love the way you pamper me and remember to always tell how much you love me with true meaning. Is that a deal?" With a sigh of relief heard around the room from the on lookers, Kelvin hugs and kisses her hungrily and whispers, "Yes, It is a deal, I promise I'll never stop pampering and love you until the day I die and beyond if possible!" Then she said most confidently,

"Yes, yes, yes, I will be your wife! I **will** marry you and make you the happiest man in the world."

He then digs into his pocket and brings out a ten karat diamond ring he was carrying around for some months and gently places it on her finger, kissing her again and again. Simultaneously, the audience cheers and wishes them good luck before returning to their dinners. In those fleeting moments her experience at age thirteen is erased. She feels like a kid again embarking on a new adventure. The excitement of the moment is so overwhelming that they couldn't finish their meal. They pick here and there, toasting to each other and accepting compliments from some of those around who want to be noticed, while one young woman who has had three failed proposals advises her not to hold her hopes too high until she catches him hook, line and sinker. "Think about this, it may be his passport to get to the prize before he owns it!" She was adamantly serious of her warning and entreats Tamina to be vigilant.

At the end of the night's adventure, Kelvin takes Tamina home as usual, they sit in the car a while longer just caressing and barely speaking, when their breaths begins to be in struggling gasps and temperatures rising, they break it off, sit a while longer to wind down, he gives her a peck on the cheek, she squeezed his hand, then decides to go into the house. He elected to stay a bit longer as he wants to visit with her parents. By this time dinner is complete, much to mama's regret. Cynthia, Tamina's mother invites him to stay for dessert. He has purchased an expensive bottle of wine and requests her parents share it with them. Curiously, Cynthia asked "What's the occasion?" Kelvin announces to her parents the good news, "Papa, Mama, for a long time I have been trying to convince your daughter to be my wife, I love her so much and need her to be with me all the way till the end of time as Mrs. Kelvin Smith. She finally agrees to marry me!" "Tamina you never told me Kelvin wanted to marry you." "That's true mama, my mind wasn't made up until today. I'll be his wife, I'll marry him!"

With adoration and praise Cynthia exclaimed, "God bless you both and I want to see grandchildren, so when you are married don't waste time, get producing." They all laughed heartily. Papa didn't say much but blessed and congratulated them. After some conversation with her parents, Kelvin announced that he is going to tell his people of this development and that he would arrange for them to come to see Tamina's parents to pay the Bride Price and arrange the traditional wedding. So after all was said, her parents excused themselves and left the room. Then following some lover's talk and caresses, Kelvin kisses her good night and left with a happy heart, anticipating the next step.

Chapter XIII

The Investigation

Stamina Lawyers is a large multi-national law firm in downtown Lagos that services mostly large businesses in Nigeria and the wider region. There is a local Division dealing with all manner of criminal and civil cases, which is Kelvin's specialty. This is what he wants to do. In early spring as Kelvin walks into his office, before he can sit at his desk, his assistant who is a paralegal brings him a file stamped **"URGENT & CONFIDENTIAL."** "As a criminal attorney I'm sure that you have seen and heard it all, especially in the United States where you had your practice," as she stops and takes a breath, "But I can assure you that you have never had a case that will challenge your very moral compass."

Raising a brow and offering a chuckle he quickly quipped "Ha... ha... ha.., I am yet to find anything in life that can make me do or feel like that."

Peering into the folder that she handed him he reads several pages then looking up staring at her and says in a calm and slow monotone, "Kindly have the family here in my office by lunch today, also contact the District Attorney and the Director of Public Prosecutions and have all related files and copies of evidence in this case sent to our offices immediately."

Kelvin feels a direct and personal interest in this case, it bothers him immensely despite that joy and happiness he displays when with Tamina. He would often say to himself, "How could a father rape his own daughter and even worse force her younger brother to do the same to her under threat?"

He couldn't find an answer. The whole issue seems to him so macabre, too distant to comprehend and too extreme for reason. Yet he has to confront it for all it's worth.

Before midday Mrs. Esther Ekeh, her thirteen year old son and her fifteen year old daughter were all present and waiting in the office board room. "Hello Mrs. Ekeh, you must be Mark and yes you're Maxine." Kelvin said stretching forth his hand welcoming them. "My name is Kelvin Smith and I am a senior partner in this law firm. I have your case, my staff will use all *available* resources of the firm to represent you and your family in this matter and in effect make sure that you are well taken care of after justice is served by putting your husband and father behind bars."

Mark is asked to leave the room while Maxine and her mother remain with Kelvin and his associate for her to give her statement. As Maxine tells vividly of the carnality of her father's actions on her, Esther cries silently only the shudders of her shoulders could have detected this, then raising her head the streams of tears are seen down her cheeks and she makes no effort to hide them. She is sorely mortified by these revelations.

Kelvin wells up with an abundance of emotions that he has to take a break from the suppressive atmosphere by getting a glass of juice he looks out the window thoughtfully and asks himself what kind of monster would do this to their own daughter? He is determined to get justice for them all, "they must be compensated for their pain and suffering this inhuman deviant inflicted upon them, we cannot allow them to become major damage goods" not realizing he was talking out loud. After a while he returns to the desk to continue taking statements.

Mark comes in after Maxine to give his statement, he is a bit uncomfortable talking about the situation in front of his mother but Kelvin reassures him that everything will be alright once he tells the truth. He relates how his father James was raping his sister frequently and instructing him to do the same while he watches under threat of physical violence. He did so reluctantly and even though he experienced natural sensations which were beyond his control it still didn't feel right as she would often be unresponsive despite his father prodding her to be an active participant.

Mrs. Ekeh has little to add to the statements as she sobs uncontrollable and continuously. "I did not know all this was going on right under my nose. Why would anyone do this to their own children? I have failed as a mother to my children!"

"This is not your fault Mrs. Ekeh, you cannot be responsible for the illicit actions of your husband, that sick bastard will pay and will get his reward from those behind bars, rape begets rape." the paralegal Allison utters.

Tamina during these weeks saw Kelvin from time to time in a state of wonderment which she couldn't comprehend, so after quizzing herself asks him why he is so distant when he's with her. He replies "This case I am doing is really worry-some but I expect it to be finished soon then we can relax again and focus my thoughts on my beautiful bride and our upcoming nuptials." After a thoughtful moment Tamina said, "Honey that's ok, you never really discussed this case with me only mention bits and pieces. Why don't you tell me more maybe I could help or at least give you my opinion from a woman's point of view?" Finally he decides to open up some more to her "Well, as I told you before this young woman Maxine, just fifteen years old is being raped by her father James who has her brother two years younger than her to do the same, under threat. James tells him he has to learn how to have sex with women so he has to start from home. Watching the boy Mark, he would usually compliment him when he is doing the right thing. Despite the protest of Mark that it's not right to have sex with his sister, James tells him to shut up and do as he says. The child would further tell his father that he thinks their mother knows what is going on and is afraid she will tell someone. James adamantly forces his will even further saying "She won't be so foolish, but if she tells anyone, I will just have them both disappear," confirming Mark's fears of what he could do to them all.

Mark runs away from home after that confrontation with his father and reports the matter to the police who respond immediately arresting James and charging him with numerous counts of rape, incest, threatening behavior, among others. Should he be convicted on all charges, James could be going to prison for life. Tamina after hearing the tragic story asks, "Who are you representing?" "I am representing Mark, Maxine and their mother". "Thank God!" "What do you mean, Thank God? Do you think I would have represented that Incestuous Criminal? As far as I am concerned, he should be castrated, locked up for life and throw away the key. How could he do such evil to his own daughter and son, his own children? I'm going to make sure he gets what coming to him." He was seething with anger and had to take command of his emotions to be able to continue the conversation with Tamina. When he was rational enough, Kelvin asked her, "What do you think honey?" Tamina is livid with anger much unlike her normal placidity.

"Do you really want to know what I think? I think that any person who rapes someone is not human at all they are simply (bleeping) cowards. They have no guts and like you said should be castrated. Of all people, **why his own daughter?** Honey I know you will do the right thing!"

Kelvin sees his objective clearly, to seek redress for their pain and suffering and more. He feels committed to bring them some comfort; though it may not wipe away all their pain, he hopes it will give them a measure of peace and a deserving new start.

Chapter XIV

The Trial

With all evidence gathered, witnesses ascertained and subpoenaed the case against James Ekeh starts one month later before Madame Justice Sarah Cafferty.   The Judge calls on the prosecutor to make his opening statements "Your honor, members of the jury I come before you today to show you how a devilish and incestuous man abused his own daughter and son under threats for them to be silent or else they would disappear. I will prove to you that James Ekeh is no more than an animal without a conscience for his behavior. Thank you, your honor."

"Defense Counsel Miss Gloria Ike, would you like to make your opening statement?"

"Yes your Honor. Mr. Ekeh is a hard-working and honest man, who takes care of his family. Mrs. Ekeh is a full time house wife and the children attend the best secondary school where they are excelling in all aspects of their education, the statements of the prosecutor are so far out of touch with reality, that I wonder why we are here. Ladies and Gentlemen of the jury you will hear that James Ekeh is a caring father who adequately protects his family, especially his vulnerable daughter.

Thank you." Then she sits down.

At this point Mr. Kelvin Smith stands up and informed the court, "I am representing the interest of the minor children Mark and Maxine Ekeh and their mother Esther Ekeh. This mother and her children have been the subject of James Ekeh's sustained cruelty and they may be adversely affected and would need certain redress."   I am going to prove to you that Mr. James Ekeh is a bad, miserable and sick individual who beats his wife and abuses his children. He then thanked the court and sits down. "Counsel, what's your name? For the record" "Kelvin Smith, I am sorry your Honor for not identifying myself!"

Justice Cafferty then directs the Prosecutor to call his first witness. "Your honor I call Mark Ekeh". The Bailiff went to the door and bellowed out "Mark Ekeh, Mark Ekeh!" after a pause then came the answer, "Yes sir, I'm coming!"

"Come this way to the witness stand."

"Put your left hand on the Bible and raise your right hand. Do you swear to tell the truth, the whole truth and nothing but the truth, so help you God?" The kid is nervous trembling and is barely audible stutters "I DO!"

With Mark on the stand, the prosecutor takes the first step to make him comfortable and allay his fears. After being satisfied that he has accomplished that goal he proceeds to have Mark tell his story. "Now Mark, in your own words, tell the court what happened."

"Well sir, I don't know when my father started having sex with my sister, one day I wanted to get a book from her so I went to her room and knocked on the door. There was no answer. So I opened the door entered the room to get the book and there I saw my father lying on top of my sister. She was crying and saying "No daddy, please stop.""

"I shouted daddy what are you doing to Maxine? He ordered me to sit down and wait until he was finished. I said no! Then he told me if I don't do as he says he will deal with me, I was so afraid that I froze and sat down there in silence with my face turned away from them and facing the wall so I couldn't see what he was doing to Maxine. When he was finished my father ordered me to take off my pants, get on top of my sister. I started to cry telling him I didn't want to. He threatened me saying that if I don't, he would go to the police and tell them he caught me having sex with my sister and the police would throw me in jail. He said I have to learn how to have sex with women and I have to start from home. I did not know what to do, so he told me to get up and he got back on Maxine and told me to look at what he was doing and watch how he moves. He got off then instructed me to get back on her and do what I saw and what he told me to. Both Maxine and I were crying. After that day daddy would drag me in Maxine's room two or three times a week for us to have sex with my sister, despite my protests. After a while I told him I think mommy knows what's going on, he said if she knows and tells anyone he would make her and Maxine disappear. That is when I ran away and reported to the police what my father was doing. I couldn't do it anymore."

When Mark had finished his evidence-in-chief the prosecutor informed the judge that he may be recalled. Justice Cafferty invites the defense counsel to cross examine if she wishes. She is eager to cross examine Mark, she starts by asking him;

"Wasn't it you your father caught having sex with your sister and you told him she gives it away to the guys out there so we should get ours too?"

"No Miss it's all a lie. That's all my father's doing!"

"Listen carefully young man, you are under oath and if you are lying to this honorable court you are liable to be sent to jail. I want you to tell the truth. When you went to your sister's room, it was not for a book you were there to have sex with Maxine willingly. There was something going on between Maxine and you, going there for a book, just an excuse for you to used? When your father caught you in the act and threatened to go to the police you ran away. Isn't that so?"

"No Miss, I did not lie to the court. What I said is exactly what happened. I have no reason to say otherwise. My father did it. I saw him!"

"You said your father forced you to have sex with your sister, tell us what happened then." "I did what he said, and then, and then…..."

    He breaks down in tears not being able to continue with the examination, the judge having compassion, excuses him from the stand. Defense Counsel reluctantly agrees. The prosecutor has made it clear he will not call the rape victim on the grounds of human compassion, he then rests his case.

The judge invites Miss Ike to call her first witness. She calls for Mr. Fred De Santis. The Bailiff swears him in and he was ready to testify.

"Now Mr. Fred tell the court how long you have known the Ekeh family."

"Madame I know Mr. Ekeh and his wife since I was five years old. We grew up together."

"Mr. Fred what kind of person is Mr. Ekeh?"

"The James Ekeh I know is an honest, decent man and would never do what he is accused of, to his own daughter? There's no way possible! My family and I enjoy a close relationship with them even Sunday dinners. Everyone was so happy. There was no indication that something was amiss."

"Thank you Mr. Fred. Your witness" The prosecutor declines.

Judge Cafferty then invites Mr. Smith to question the witness. "Thank you your Honor.

Now Mr. Fred you said Mr. Ekeh is an honest and decent man. Are you honest and decent?"

"Yes sir!"

"Now tell me something, when you and your best friend James Ekeh were fifteen years old, weren't you arrested for beating and raping a young woman?" "Yes sir, but we were exonerated."

"Not because you were not guilty, but because the victim in question was afraid to testify against you. She was threatened that if she testifies her whole family would die. So she kept silent. That was the only reason why you got off. Your honor, this man is not a reliable witness." The judge then inquired if any other lawyer needed to examine him, all declined and he was instructed to step down, but keep himself available to be called again if needed.

The case continues as Miss Ike calls the accused to the stand. He's sworn in and she begins to lead him in his testimony.

"Mr. Ekeh, tell us in your own words what happened."

"Madame, I came home one day from work not feeling well, my wife was not home, I didn't expect anyone else to be home as my children would have been in school. But habitually I would check the rooms of the house. When I got to my daughter's room I heard sobbing, I listened more closely then I opened the door to find my son Mark on top of my daughter. She was crying telling him to get off. I grabbed him by the arm and pulled him off her. That is when he told me that she gives it to the guys at school, so it is better if I have it too!"

Mark and Maxine jump from their seats shouting, "Liar, liar you did it all." The young woman starts sobbing again, the audience murmuring and the judge called for order in the court tapping her gavel and ordering the children to sit. They did. Miss Ike informs the court she had no more witnesses and rested her case.

Judge Cafferty enquires if anyone of the other attorneys wanted to cross examine James. The prosecutor declined. Kelvin replies "Not now your honor." James was then asked to step down.

"Mr. Smith, do you have any witnesses?"

"Yes your honor, I call Mr. Mark Ekeh to the stand. Mark you are still under oath and are required to testify to the truth. Mark, when you came to my office you gave my assistant something, which I hoped I wouldn't have to use. Your honor this is a DVD I would like the court to enter into evidence as exhibit 'A.'" The Bailiff hastily takes the disc from Mr. Smith and gives it to the judge who examines the cover and allows it into evidence, marking it as exhibit "A."

The Defense counsel objects.

"Your honor we did not know anything of this evidence."

"Well, you know now and I said I will allow it. So sit down let's get on with the case."

Then Kelvin Continues, "Your honor, if there are any children in the courtroom please have them removed as the contents of this DVD we are about to view is very graphic." The judge so orders them cleared from the courtroom. The Bailiff inserts the

DVD into the player, when the video starts Mr. Ekeh is seen walking into his daughter's room, approaching her, he's starting to disrobe saying "Come on girl, the past times you were not participating as you should. You have to move your hips to show you are a real woman, not lie down like a log." "Daddy what are you talking about?" You know what to do!" Slapping her across the face knocking her down on the bed. She jumps up immediately rubbing her face in disbelief. "Listen girl, I give you everything in this house; I need some kind of a reward." He rips her clothes off leaving her stark naked, crying and pleading,

"Daddy please don't I am tired of you doing this to me and having Mark doing it too against his will."

"Girl, shut up!" Grabbing her by the upper arms throws her across the bed again while quickly finishing disrobing, gets on top of her and proceeds to have sex as she is protesting all the while. Completing his immorality he threatens her again, "Remember, if you say one word to anyone you and your mother **will disappear**." He is then seen leaving her room with his clothes in hand.

"Your honor, Maxine enlisted the assistance of her brother in placing a streaming webcam in her room to document her ordeal. She found this to be necessary after the constant abuse and threats from her father to make her and her mother disappear should anyone find out. Look as she is crying hysterically after he leaves saying out loud but sounding a bit inaudible "I don't know how much more I can take maybe I should run away but where would I go, I don't know anyone elsewhere." See she falls to her knees and cries more painfully "God please help me let this be the end of it."" Mr. Smith is heartily please with the video and his presentation he is jubilant in announcing to the judge, "Your honor, I rest my case!"

The judge is shocked by the evidence just presented calls on the prosecutor to cross examine Mark to which he responds "Your Honor, I have no further need to cross examine this witness."

Laboring under shared disgust the judge then calls on Miss Ike for her turn to cross examine the witness and she responds holding her head bowed "Your honor I have no questions for this witness but would ask the court for a one day recess to rebut this evidence" the judge responds "your client has had amply enough time to advise you correctly on the matter so your request is a waste of the courts time and money. YOUR REQUEST IS DENIED!"

The Judge at this point calls on all parties to proceed with their closing arguments. The prosecutor begins his closing statement saying "The people are extremely happy by the evidence that was presented before this honorable court. We have nothing more to say or needs saying to this impaneled jury to gain a conviction especially after the video. "Mr. Smith your closing statement". "Ladies and Gentlemen of the jury the DVD speaks for itself. This man should not be let out on the street to rape any more young women. If he could do it to his own daughter he can do it to anyone's child out there even yours. Thank You."

The case is over in two weeks but not before becoming national headlines in all publications digital and print. Kelvin is sought after for interviews and his advice to others in similar situations. He is also offered several ministerial positions with the Federal Government of Nigeria to which he gracefully declines stating that his true love of the law is based on helping the less fortunate individuals in society with the ultimate goal of a better person and a better world.

As expected James Ekeh is convicted and sentenced to life on the most serious charge; the lesser charges drew the maximum sentences. The Judge expresses her disgust for such conduct and all the circumstances surrounding the crimes. She then orders therapy for the children and their mother for an initial six month period which could be extended according to the progress made. Kelvin then makes an application to the court to seek redress for damages from the estate of Mr. Ekeh to aid them in restarting their lives. The judge notes the application and scheduled a date for a hearing, pending report from the government's social agencies.

James now has his own problems going into prison to deal with the other inmates who have learnt of the case and its outcome. Many of them have daughters whom they love. "Mom, let's see how he feels being raped by men," was the painful expression of Maxine, she visibly seem to be relieved at the outcome and holds on to her mother. Mark apologizes to his mother and sister both accepted because they knew the circumstances under which he acted.

They are on their way to begin a new life without fear. Kelvin is relieved and wishes them good luck on their journey back to civilization. It appears there are not enough words to thank Kelvin so the trio just hugs him and wept. He had a difficult time controlling himself so as not to join them. After they had come to a point of satisfaction they let him go with tear stains on the suit which he so loved but he wore it proudly as a badge of honor.

Chapter XV

The Grand Affair

    With the case now behind him Kevin has time to concentrate on his upcoming nuptials much to the delight of Tamina. Preparations are in place, guests invited, foods, refreshments and special delights are all taken care of; their big day has arrived with much pomp and circumstance. It becomes a grand affair where all the state dignitaries and the who's who of his social circle would be seen since his popularity is still in full swing from the notoriety of his big case.

Tamina wants a Church Wedding while Kelvin wants a Traditional ceremony so they both had their satisfaction. After the Church wedding in her bridal gown and he in his American cut suit they went home and change for the traditional affair.

Their traditional wedding is one of the biggest seen in Lagos in decades. The women are elegantly dressed in lavish tribal attire with magnificent head dresses that in some cases diminish their faces. Head dress and the wraps in the society are significant to a woman's fashion. They spare no pains making them as elaborate as possible to look their best. The men in new colorful caps which proudly depicted their station of the chieftain rank and the elders on both sides make sure their presence will not be overshadowed, they take every opportunity to ensure not to be forgotten while drinking the traditional palm wine and eating the kola nuts.

Custom means everything in Nigeria especially at the wedding ceremony, as tradition dictates Tamina who is lavishly dressed in her native wedding regalia must first find her husband who is similarly dressed and seated among the crowd of men and present him with the ceremonial drink in a traditional vessel at the commencement of the ceremony which will indicate this is her love… the one she will be marrying. The festivity continues with joyful celebration leading up to the much anticipated welcoming to the family by the couple's parents.

First is Tamina's father, who begins by saying "To my wonderful daughter who has not had the easiest life, you never gave up when things were hard, when the trials came to you, you made the right choices. When it looked dark and there was no light at the end of the tunnel you still navigated through it all. From a child you blossomed into a wonderful woman with a brilliant education blooming into a well-respected medical doctor. Instead of remaining in the U.S. you returned home to help your people with all your talents. I love you my darling. Mr. Smith, this lady will make you a great man so it's on you to be her loving husband tending to her needs as required. In all just love her for whom she truly is. Today I say welcome to my family son."

Up next is Kelvin's mother as is father who would normally stand in for him is late. "To my son you are everything that a mother could ever want in a child. From your birth I always knew that you were going to be a great man today as you now take another wife, a Nigerian wife I hope that the happiness that I shared with your father would be yours totally. Tamina I say welcome to our family and get busy I need plenty grand-children before I go to join my ancestors."

The couple decided that Kelvin would speak for them both. "Thank you all for joining us today witnessing our love for each other. Tamina and I know that life can change in an instant, that's why we seize the moment, that opportunity to embark on our voyage through life. Our happiness together will be the wind in our sails. So my friends eat, drink and be merry. That is, have as much dessert as you want... Ha, ha, ha!"

The master of ceremonies then shouts out to the crowd, "To the bride and groom" and with a thunderous yell and glasses raised they saluted the newlyweds.

Foreign wines and liquors are consumed particularly by the younger generation who do not crave the traditional palm wine. When dancing the guests are showering the newlyweds with dollars as the drummers set the rage with their contagious rhythm. The scantily dressed gyrating tribal dancers never seem to tire. The longer they danced the more ready they were to continue, even outlasting many particularly the more senior folk.

As the festivities wind down and some of the elders unable to sustain the long fluid filled hours begins falling asleep while others are taken to their cars by concerned sons or other family members and a few are trying to compete with the young men drinking foreign wines, liquors and palm wine or a concoction of it all. Even trying to pick up the vivacious young women who are prancing about, many clothed in Western style mini dresses which expose most of their assets and much of their pride attributes which the older women jealously protect under long well accented dresses, seeking to make them their second wife and bragging how wealthy they are even promising they can inherit all of their riches.

During this time the newlywed couple slips away being chauffeured off to their honeymoon villa on Lake Ecumba, in the North of the country. Cleo and Cynthia spent significant time picking up all the money showered on them filling two large duffel bags which they take into the house for safe keeping.

After one month of blissful conjugal happiness they return to reality. Tamina moves into Kelvin's home in the Western suburbs. He has had this house for some time but now it would be their new home.

The Smiths' are having the happiest time of their lives with no children on the way they made a carefully thought decision to firstly enjoy each other to the fullest, with their new found freedom. Life is oh so good.

Chapter XVI

First Responder

About one year after their glorious wedding day something strange happened much to Tamina's surprise. Towards the end of the work day the night staff is reporting for duty while she and the day staff are preparing to leave. She is about to exit her office and is distracted by the sound of loud voices of people shouting, some crying, while others are begging not to be shot. Realizing that there is a commotion in one of the rooms in the facility, she decides to investigate the source.

She calmly puts her bags down walks out of the office and locks the door placing the keys in her pocket then proceeds cautiously to the scene of the noise. When she reaches the room she stops outside the door listens for a while trying to assess the situation, she opens the door just a crack enabling her to view the entire room where some twenty patients and staff are lying on the floor being held at gun point by three thugs. The cashier is the only person sitting in her cage where all the day's receipts are kept. She's handed a large canvas bag and given orders to fill it with money and drugs from the secure cabinet. Tamina tries to close the door but not before she is spotted by one of the gun men. She tries to run but this fleet footed fellow caught up and grabbed her about the neck with his left arm holding the weapon in his right hand.

A struggle ensues with Tamina knocking the gun from his grip the weapon firing when it struck the floor sending the bullet wildly ricocheting off the walls and floor. She goes to work on this hapless fellow, treating him to the finest of her martial arts skills, kicking and tossing him about like a rag doll until he was out on his feet. She retrieves the gun, then drags him into the last room at the end of the corridor where she sat him down on a chair, ties and gags him, at this point he is still out cold. Getting her faithful baseball bat as a support device she returns to the door where she was looking into the main room where the people are being held hostage. Some begin crying even more as they think she is shot and killed as the sound came from the direction of her office. Turning their attention back to the room with the hostages the two remaining gun men discuss briefly and laughing, "That bitch is dead!" after which demanding silence of the group or they'll suffer the same fate. One of the crooks was instructed by his apparent leader to keep surveillance on the hostages and to shoot anyone who tries anything. With this taken care of, he again turns his attention back to the cashier threatening her to hurry up and fill the bags with drugs from the storage room and the money from the register.

"Move faster you useless woman before I put a bullet in yo; yo too slow!"

It has been over five minutes since the first thug left the room and nothing is heard of him since the gun fired, this worries the leader who instructs the other thug saying

"Lonzo….. Go see what happen to Raffi man."

Lonzo following the instruction calls out "Raffi! Raffi! Wha yo doing back there so long? I tho't yo finish that bitch off, let's go!"

But he gets no answer from Raffi. Walking down the corridor still calling for Raffi to no avail he begins checking the rooms. Slowly closing in on the last room he notices that door is ajar, he pushes the door boldly open, seeing Raffi chair bound in the center of the room, he rushes in only to be disarmed by Tamina who is standing behind the door. She executes an accurately sharp blow with her baseball bat on the gun hand causing the weapon to fall from his grip, before the surprise could dissipate she proceeds to kick, stomp and chop him with such precision and expertise that in a short while Lonzo was out cold too. She ties him to another chair, gagging him as a precaution, then affixing the chairs back to back and binding them together, avoiding any attempt to escape should they recover. Here's to her victory two thieves down and secured she is satisfied then she calls the police. Still Tamina didn't even break a sweat.

While waiting for the police, Tamina walks into the main room where the last gunman is still awaiting his friends' return and is agitated since it seems that they are taking too long to accomplish the simple task of putting away a mere woman. He is calling for them but couldn't get a response as they are out of ear shot and out cold.

She is carrying her faithful baseball bat tucked under her arm along with the two guns from the bound robbers. Tamina quietly enters the waiting room and speaks startling him; he turns around at the sound of her voice.

"Drop your weapon, NOW!"

"And if I don't, what will you do?" He was daring her to challenge him.

"Don't be stupid I have two guns and your friends are out of commission. Do you want a beating or to be shot?"

"You are just a stupid useless woman do you think I will allow you to beat me, BITCH?"

"Let's put it to the test. We will both put down our guns together." They did so simultaneously, kicking them away and stood back to fight.

He is a large man about six feet six inches tall and weighs over two hundred pounds, while Tamina is only five feet five inches and weighs just about one hundred and forty pounds. However despite his size she is confident he's no match for her and knows she can take him out.

He feels good when he considers the odds in his favor and threw the first punch; Tamina steps back and sideways to her left parrying the blow and trapping his arm in a lock bringing him down.

He hits the floor with a thud so hard that it echoes across the room. She adeptly disengages and stands back ready for the next assault. He is now more humiliated than hurt, his anger flares as he rushes Tamina to execute a bear hug. Again she side steps him and sends him flying into a corner with a well delivered chop behind the neck. **Now he is really angry with nasals flaring and eyes glaring** he decides to be more cautious, to use more strength to catch and subdue her. So faking a move to his right Tamina side steps to her right he then move to his left quickly confident he had entrapped her. So crouching, coming head first at her in a position he feels convinced that she couldn't evade him, she stoops and moves left, pulling his legs at the same time sending him crashing into the wall head first. She then gets on him with strategic kicks to the neck, groin and nose, twisting his arm to a position he didn't know it have been bent, then beating his knees with her ever present bat. He tries to retaliate, standing up she happily introduces him to a series of flips and throws the last of which he lands on his head by this time **he is screaming for help**. She still didn't break a sweat.

The police arrived several minutes into the crisis and following Tamina's given directions they enter the facility through a rear door where they locate the two bound individuals she had subdued they are immediately arrested. Following the loud noise they came upon the lobby where they stood in the doorway with mouths agape in awe watching this little woman trashing this huge man and enjoying every moment of it since they could not have done a better job themselves. When he saw the police, he begins begging them to take him away, rescue him before she kills him. He is so disoriented, bruised and bleeding he didn't believe that, this little woman could inflict so much pain on him, the mighty village wrestling champion Ellis Ameka.

As the police are taking them away Tamina stops them for one last bit of warning. "To you and your friends The Tamina Health Center is **Off LIMITS!**

The next time you come here, you wouldn't get off so easily. Officers, Take them away please….!"

"Come on let's go, you useless criminals, MOVE!" With Lonzo crying, "She bruk m' han',"

As the arresting officers are leaving Kelvin comes to the main room. He has been calling Tamina without success so he decides to visit the center to find out what is happening.

He is alarmed to see the large contingent of policemen at the center and the three men in handcuffs being taken away.

"What's going on here?" he asks Tamina. But before she could answer the Inspector compliments him saying

"Barrister!" slapping him on the shoulder, "If I had a wife like yours every place I go she will be at my side and I will never let her go!" "What are you talking about?"

"Ask your wife."

"Honey, what's wrong?" Even more perplexed.

"Sweet heart those guys came in, held us up and tried to rob us and we defended ourselves." She says most casually.

Her sister Cleo excitedly said, "Brotha, you have no idea what a powerful woman you are married to! She took on those three armed robbers bare handed!"

"What! Honey you could have been killed!"

Another nurse says, "First they would have to ambush her to kill her!" "Enough of that, I was just trying to protect us. Now you guys can lock up the place and go home or go back to work, whatever you choose to do. I'm going home. Darling let's go home so you can make love to your wife, after that dreadful ordeal." This happened to be amusing to the whole staff, which was standing there.

"You will have to tell me more about what happened."

"Sure honey, later."

"Good night all!" She grabs her husband's arm and they leave THE TAMINA HEALTH CENTER with the night shift in charge.

While on the drive home they do not say much however Tamina is lost in her fantasy of expectation and is deeply engrossed in her thoughts.

Arriving home Kaaren the gate person opens the gate Kelvin parks the car as usual in the second parking bay, she closes the gate and takes the bags from the car into the house, following Kelvin and Tamina who are in each other's arms as usual.

Dinner is the most important meal to Kelvin. He has never looked at his wife in this light before they were married. There is a bit of mystery, admiration and downright thought of foolishness at what she did. He wonders if this little woman his woman his tender loving woman could have performed the feats described to him and come out unscathed. He is too confused to even smile, too concerned too numb to imagine what could have been. Is he being too melodramatic? Dinner ends on a somber note.

Tamina is preparing for bed when she takes extra care to create the atmosphere which would seduce him not as usual but for the animal in him to hungrily need her to soothe his throbbing rigid passion, to give her the redress so deserving a conqueress in the privacy of la chambre de couche. She has a flashing memory of that fateful day when she was ravaged and feels great exercising her authority for the first time in Nigeria since that rape. She feels **victory** against the violence that deprived her of the most cherished possession, chastity. Here she is eagerly preparing to enjoy the most sacred of human intimacy in amorous fashion, knowing it would not be the same experience as when she was thirteen.

Finally they get into bed at their favorite spots and turning off the lights, Tamina expecting a great reward for her heroic anticipating the fireworks and cannons exploding when they make love tonight arriving at the simultaneous climax, then spontaneously reaching for a return to reality.

Breathing in deep lung filled breathes, then in staccato hisses, mouth wide open, eyes closed and anything said seems not to make sense, scratching clawing pinching and biting with him having to control her twisting and contorting body when the ecstatic unction, that long flood of satisfaction is uncontrollably excreting collapsing her into a limp helpless mess. She turns to him smiling kissing his neck nibbling on his ears caressing his nipples then working her way down caressing his upper thigh slipping her hand into his crotch grabbing the tool of satisfaction announcing her expectation. She succeeds to a point. Kelvin gives the best he could have under the circumstances and she falls asleep thereafter. He is more concerned of how close he came to losing her. "Oh Lord, please don't take another wife away from me!" He embraces her as she lies asleep and pleads in tearful earnestness before he falls into a fitful sleep.

Rarely do they have the opportunity most mornings to sit and have breakfast with each other, but the morning after Tamina instructs Brenda to prepare their favorite meal over which they will sit and enjoy to the fullest, it is only then that Tamina tells him exactly what had happened that previous afternoon at the Center and how she was able to restore order for her staff and patients' sake.

"You didn't have to worry honey. I was in perfect control at all times the mere surprise was my biggest and best ally."

"My Dear Tammy you didn't have to do that, please leave it to the professionals. Do you realize you could have been killed? I have lost one wife to recklessness I don't want to be a widower a second time. You mean the world to me I will be totally broken if anything takes you away from me. Promise me that you will never do any such thing again. You promise?" She feeling his pain as she heard him and read his eyes suddenly something in her heart felt submission like she never felt it before. But she retorted "Hon, I know I must have been a bit over the edge doing what I did but had the police come in before me there would have been a stand-off and hostages taken even people killed. My actions saw no lives lost and the criminals arrested but to be the good wife if ever it happens again I'll definitely call the police. I promise!" with her fingers crossed behind her back. How relieved he is to have her word and he feels confident she would keep it. "But honey, where did you learn to do that?" "Oh, I had a few lessons on how to defend myself if needed."

Feeling exhausted from her significant dual performances Tamina decides to head back to her boudoir to get some well deserve rest and to reflect on the manner in which she took control of the situation at the center last night noting vocally "As a child I could never stand up to defend myself even for my chastity, but now as a woman I took down three big men who wanted to create that nightmare by my being unable to defend myself. I've won and they've lost it all this time. My reward is that sensual pleasure from the best man in the entire world. I've never felt love like that before…. Ahhh. Its times like these it is good to be the boss. I think I would sleep in today. She then called the center, telling the secretary to cancel all of her appointments since she wouldn't be in. I need to recuperate and I deserve it."

Chapter XVII
Just send them away

Two days later while in her office reviewing important paper work she is interrupted by a sharp knock on the door.

"Come in!" The nurse steps in and with some concern says to her "Doctor, there are two ladies here to see you."

"Who are they, what do they want? Tell them I am busy and can't see anyone right now maybe tomorrow! Just send them away!"

"I think they are two of the women who were held up by the armed robbers the other day."

"They thanked me already, what else do they want?" displaying some annoyance.

"I don't know Doctor, but they insist they have to see you today!"

"OK," Resignedly, "Tell them to come in. I'll give them just fifteen minutes. You must come back at that time calling me for an emergency patient, so I can get the rid of them. Show them in. Thank you!"

The two women enter the office but before they greet Tamina they are surveying the room approvingly, and then say to her,

"Good day madam!"

"Good day to you and welcome!" The first woman, the tall statuesque one with long hair well done and adorned spoke,

"We had to come back to see you and to thank you once more still this is not nearly enough!"

"But ladies you did so already!"

"Yes!" said the other, the shorter of the two whose attire was most immaculate, with matching head dress. Tamina is not opposed to traditional dress, but prefers the western garbs she is so accustom to wearing. "We know, but after leaving we realized that we may know you!" "Know me!" She says with great element of surprise. "OK, you mean by coming to the clinic?"

"No!" said the first woman. That day was the first time we ever came to the clinic. Someone recommended it to us. My name is Stella and she's Mami. Does this ring a bell?"

Tamina reflecting remembers the names and that fateful day now more than thirty years ago when her friends bearing the same names ran away leaving her in a situation from hell.

"Yes, when I was young I had two friends, two best friends who deserted me when I needed them most. It can't be, oh my God is it you two?" Enthusiastically she leaps from behind her desk knocking over several files in the process then clinging to each other in a most emotional hug; they jumping up like preteen girls and shedding tears of joy, sorrow and remorse. When the tears subside Mami's head dress is on the floor but they didn't care about that she wants to hear from Tamina. "We are so sorry that we ran away from you on that horrible day we were so scared; we didn't know what happened and you stopped coming to school. When we decided to look for you we were told you had traveled." Stella on her knees, Mami follows and Stella speaks to Tamina haltingly, in deep emotion and grief,

"Tamina, can you ever forgive us?" By this time they were all bitterly crying and Mami is muttering something inaudible. Tamina is firm with them,

"Get up. You don't have to kneel to me. I have forgiven you a long time ago. I am at peace and you must now do the same. Let's sit and chat. Would you like something to drink? Better yet, let's go out to lunch!"

As arranged Nurse Ibo enters the office but before she could speak Tamina takes the initiative "Nurse Ibo, my friends and I are going out to lunch. These ladies and I grew up together but over the years lost touch with each other. How strange the ways you find lost friends. You know how to get me if there is an emergency!"

Lunch is a gratifying experience. They have thirty something years to catch up on, Stella and Mami both told her they are married to successful men in the import and export business, they also have their own businesses. Stella owns a Beauty Salon, Mami a Boutique and they all are doing well. They have happy lives and two children each a boy and girl who are now away at the university. Stella's boy was pursuing Chemical Engineering while his sister was reading Law and both of

Mami's children are pursuing medicine. No one asked Tamina of children and she didn't volunteer to say. All she said was "Well girls, you know who I am and that my husband is Barrister Smith. "You mean THE BARRISTER SMITH?" They said in unison. "Yes the one and only."

Following that day of so long ago my parents sent me to my aunt and uncle in America. I went to school there pursued studies and became a doctor. I own The Tamina Health Center and am giving back to the community. It has been too long since we have been apart. Are you in touch with others with whom we grew up? It would be so nice to see them today I am sure they are all doing well."

After the meal, a few glasses of good wine for Mami and Stella and much talk Tamina is preparing to take her leave "I have to get back to the office. I must complete a report for the government which must be filed tomorrow. As business women I know you will understand, let's exchange contact information our numbers and addresses and such. I can drop you back to your offices on my way!"

"Thank you very much but that wouldn't be necessary. Our drivers were behind us all the way and we will go with them. Thanks again!"

"You are welcome!" Hugging and saying their goodbyes, Tamina reminds them to keep in touch and they reply "We will, you can count on it!"

Kelvin and Tamina are so happy it seems the honeymoon will never end. They are involved with their businesses and amply so with each other, that they would finish the other's sentences as though they were linked with one mind. She tells Kelvin what happened at the center with her two friends, he calls it unbelievable. "You mean that after thirty something years you meet because of an armed robbery? Unbelievable!" "That's not all; I invited them and their husbands to dinner one night. You will get to meet them!" "That's nice I will look forward to meeting these mysterious old friends!"

Chapter XVIII

Mother-in-Law Venom

Three years of marriage they still had no children much to the disappointment of her mother-in-law. They would try to comfort her by saying when God is ready, in God's own time we will have children, to which they would often hear

"Either you are not trying hard enough or God is punishing you for something you did in the past" To this they are often amused, laughing out loudly.

Few things ever disrupt the peace and tranquility of the Smith's domain and such issues are merely trivial annoyances. One such annoyance was Kelvin's mother, who becomes a major disruption.

Tamina heading home one day not particularly tired but enough to anticipate a special form of unwinding. She is thinking of swimming, to be totally free to have the evening air fan her cheeks with her hair opened to length and she envisions the pool lights wrapping her entire form casting long shadows when she clambers onto the diving board, then relaxing, sitting on an inflated tube in her pool to savor the mood of the day and the thoughts of her husband. By the time she gets to that point of the fancy she arrives home, but not to what she is expecting.

She parks her car in the first bay as usual, takes her pocket book while Kaaren takes her other bags into the house. Kaaren, is six feet two inches tall and weighs about two hundred and forty pounds, very shapely and beautiful, a man's desire.

When Tamina enters the front room her entire evening is shattered for sitting there is her mother-in-law Naomi and sister-in-law Ifoma.

Utterly surprised, she couldn't speak for a moment. "Mama, Ifoma, what's going on? I didn't know you were coming. Kelvin didn't tell me!" Tamina is trying to figure out why her in-laws are in her home. Brenda one of the house help comes in takes her attaché and the other bags away to her study. Kelvin comes in singing as usual his praises to Tamina. She is perplexed as she had no prior knowledge of this development. Her attitude is not pleasant and makes no effort to conceal how she feels, for when Kelvin is serenading her she raises her right hand stopping him.

"Now what's going on here? You never told me your mother was coming! How could you just have them show up here without first discussing it with me?"

"Oh honey, my honey!" getting close to her and putting his arms around her. "I was told that mama is sick I told them to come next weekend so I can take her to the doctor and that would have given me enough time to discuss the issue with you."

"No Kelvin, you had made up your mind already. What would you have done if I didn't agree to have them? Would you have called them back to tell them they couldn't come? Then I would appear to be the bad bitch and your mother would have hated me for depriving her of your love!" "That was not intended and mama would never hate you!

I'm sorry, but I know the loving person that you are, you wouldn't have said no to my mother, your mother-in-law." "Never the less, you can talk to me about anything at any

172

future time. We did talk about everything before, so don't stop now." "Alright Tammy honey, I will definitely remember that!" Then kissing her on the cheeks and about her neck which she loves, she begins to respond as she normally does until mama clears her throat to remind them she is still there. This is evidence enough that she has forgiven him.

Two weeks passes and mama is still here even though she has seen the doctors, gotten her medication and is fully recovered. She thinks to herself, why should I go back to the village when my son who has plenty of money and this big house, he can maintain me here, instead of spending all his money on that barren woman his wife, then talking to Ifoma saying "She hasn't giving me any grandchildren. He must take a second wife." Unknown to her
Tamina overhears the discussion with Ifoma of Kelvin taking a second wife to give her grandchildren, but says nothing, not even to Kelvin.

During this period Tamina is in no way rude, disrespectful or aggressive towards her in-laws but respectfully sees that they are comfortable. Now mama is confident she has seen everything she wants to see and in her view Kelvin is bewitched by Tamina. She decides to talk to her son "Kelvin my son, you must take a second wife, and send away that barren witch you call your wife. She doesn't want to give me grandchildren because she doesn't want to lose her **Yankee figure** having children." Kelvin tries to explain to his mother that "We love each other and want to have children, I don't want a second wife; it has been only three years since we are married and when God is ready we will have children." The matter did not rest there, for his mother feels since her talk with him did not bear the fruit she expects, she must take matters into her own hands immediately.

Some days later Tamina comes home greets Naomi who does not return the greeting instead unleashing a tirade upon her,

"Look at you, all you good for is to spend my son's money and would not give him a child!" To avoid disrespect Tamina does not banter words with her as she expects but simply walks away. She is quite upset at the unnecessary and unfair attack volleying against her but holds her peace

Kaaren and two house help Gloria and Brenda are there since Kelvin and Tamina were married. The Smiths are happy with their performance and have no plans to replace them. They keep the compound secure and clean the house exceptionally clean and spotless their meals cooked daily fresh and tasty the way they enjoy it. Everything in their household works until mama thinks differently.

When Kelvin and Tamina head off to their respective businesses mama searches the house and compound. What she is hoping to find no one knows but she searches and asks questions of Gloria and Brenda to which they cannot give an answer. She isn't particularly fond of them though she thinks Gloria would have been a good second wife for Kelvin if she wasn't a house girl. She admires how she cleans the house and washes clothes; mama holds the fantasy in her mind never making mention to anyone her innermost feelings. Despite this she distances herself from both women and could be seen and heard bullying them around.

After making her rounds one day, she sits down under a shady tree in the compound to analyze all she has seen. Mama then decides that two house helpers are too much they don't do enough. She declares herself the boss and from this day on she will tell them what to do.

She gives Gloria all of her clothes to wash some of which didn't need washing. Demanding that her room be swept twice a day and her bed linens change whenever the bed is made. She also wants her curtains changed and washed weekly.

Brenda did not have it any easier for she was required to clean the kitchen walls and floor, washing the dishes, pots and pans as well as the bathrooms in the house daily, she must also accompany her on walks whenever she so desires. When all these things are done she would insist upon Kaaren to sweep the compound twice daily. She really makes their lives miserable.

The final decision she makes tops everything else, she instructs them to stop their cooking of all meals. Several days before this decision is made the help cooks dinner "Madam your dinner is ready!" Then giving her the tray of food when she sits in her favorite chair where she eats alone. She looks at the food and said "This is what you call food?" throwing the tray with the food at the girl hitting her squarely in the face and splattering down the front of her clothes causing her minor scalds. This was followed by an illicit and angry beating of Brenda instructing her not to cook anymore that she must leave the cooking to the Madame.

That day mama ate nothing when she is around the girls but quietly goes to her room and eats from a supply she has stacked away. The girls feel some relief at her absence only it is short lived before she returns to continue her assault upon them. Never telling Tamina what she has done but she continues to torment the girls until it is near the time of Tamina's return from work.

The next day starts as usual with one major exception, Tamina tells Brenda not to prepare breakfast for Kelvin and herself as they would have it at their favorite restaurant in the city. Just prepare breakfast for Ifoma and mama who heard the instruction but say nothing.

When Brenda was finished preparing the meal and informed mama she waves her off and refuses to touch it, but later that morning she takes juice from the refrigerator and drank a large glass then demanded that Gloria wash the glass she has just finish using. No food is cooked that day Gloria and Brenda did their cleaning and clothes washing as mama dictates and ate fu-fu they had saved from yesterday night.

Tamina comes home that evening looking forward to the usual hot tasty meal with her husband. She is utterly surprised to find that there is no meal prepared despite the fact there is every ingredient in the house to do so.

"Brenda, Gloria!" She calls with mild anger.

"Yes Auntie." "What happened why isn't my meal prepared?"

"Mama told me not to cook anymore. I must leave all the cooking to you Auntie," replies Brenda

"When did she tell you so?"

"Yesterday, she said I mustn't cook anymore Auntie you will."

"Oh I see I'll have a talk with her. Thank you."

When Tamina turns around she didn't have to go far to find mama. Surprised as she is to find mama behind her she tries desperately to conceal it and maintain her decorum.

"Mama, you're welcome."

"Who is your Mama? You usually come home at 5 pm it's now 7 pm. Where in hell were you? Don't you know that you have to come home and prepare dinner for me?"

"Mama, what do you mean? That's what the house help is here for." "The house help can't cook for me. Today is my Birthday and I want something special!"

"Well Mama I'll call Kelvin and have him bring home something special for us to eat. I am very tired and all I need to do right now is a bath and go straight to ….!"

Tamina did not finish the statement, she had intended to say "bed" Kelvin's mother planted herself squarely in her path blocking the way so she could not pass. Surprisingly she delivers a stinging slap across Tamina's face then forcefully instructs her,

"Get in the kitchen and cook me something to eat, I don't want restaurant food. I want a good dish for my birthday and **you** Tamina will cook it you barren useless woman!" Then turning to Ifoma, "You see what I told you all she wants to do is spend my son, your brother's money. Useless woman can't even give me a grandchild!"

Tamina is more surprise than hurt by the assault made upon her she's trying hard to maintain her dignity and respect for her mother-in-law. Instead of retaliating she takes a rather passive stance.

Tamina cries she has not done so for more than twenty years she almost forgets she has tears but mama brings them back. She holds her face with her left hand with tears streaming down her cheeks; she decides to address her mother-in-law. In utter disbelief of what has just happened Tamina softly retorts

"Mama you slapped me?"

"Yes!!!! And I will slap you again if you don't get in that kitchen and prepare me something to eat now." With dismay and total restraint Tamina issues a stern warning

"Let me tell you something Mama I have total respect for you because you are my husband's mother, you are my mother-in-law but the next time you put your hands on me I will teach you and your daughter a lesson you will never forget. I am warning you **please don't**

ever hit me again!" When she finishes her warning to both women she lifts her head with tears still flowing down her face she sees Kelvin standing at the door with his hands on his hips she had no idea how long he was there. Kelvin did not see the slap when he walked in,

"What is going on here Tamina?"

"Nothing is going on!" She is very upset and still crying.

"What do you mean nothing? I came in and heard you threatening Mama and Ifoma" through all this Kelvin did not notice his wife crying.

Mama speaks hurriedly and convincingly "My son, my son, you see, you see how disrespectful she is to me and your sister. I am telling you let her pack her bags and get out, and bring another wife in here so she can give you children!"

"Mama Tamina will not disrespect you unless you did something to her." Tamina gave mama a nasty look rolling her eyes and shaking her head in disbelief walking away she goes upstairs to the solace of her bedroom to think and calm herself down, she just wants to be left alone in her own world.

The conversation continues as Kelvin tries to ascertain what happened and why. There is quite a lot of talk going nowhere then suddenly Gloria one of the help shouted

"She slapped Auntie!"

"What! What did she do to deserve a slap? Now listen to me carefully the next time you hit my wife you and Ifoma will be out of this house and back to the village. Regardless of what may have happened you have no right to slap my wife!"

"Kelvin you are throwing me and your sister, out for that tramp, that useless woman!"

"Mama I have spoken! Now I brought home a special dinner for your birthday." Then turning to the house help,

 "Here Brenda, put this on the table!"
"Oh my son you remembered!"

"Of course I must remember my Mother's birthday, Happy Birthday Mom! But I'm still upset with you for hitting my wife." He then gives her an envelope.

"Mom here is Two Hundred Thousand Naira. You and Ifoma can go shopping tomorrow."

"Thank you my son, thank you!!"

She is smiling from ear to ear in a most comical and contagious manner. Then hugging Kelvin and snuggling up to him contently.

   Kelvin then goes upstairs apologizes for himself and mother, pleading with his wife to forgive them. "Please come downstairs to celebrate mama's birthday with us."

Despite all that took place Tamina had dinner with the family and is totally ignored by Naomi, Kelvin ignoring that position mentions to his wife what he told mama and promises that it would be enforced.

"No one will ever come to this home and make any of us unhappy. Not even you mama!" Dinner ended with them singing Happy Birthday to Mama.

Chapter XIX

The Visit

The ensuing weeks are uneventful to say the least during which time Tamina gets a phone call from her Aunt and Uncle in America

"Hi Auntie, how are you?"

"We are ok, but we have a surprise for you."

"Yes, what is it?" with excitement in her voice.

"We're coming to visit Nigeria!"

"We're going to bring Carl and Cindy too?"

"Yes all of us, also Iyke."

"Is Samantha coming with Iyke?"

"No. When we get there we'll talk about her!"

"When exactly are you coming?"

"In three weeks. We will call you with the flight information so you can pick us up at the Airport."

Tamina is so *happy* she begins jumping for joy, taking a minute to catch her breath she shares with her in-laws that her relatives from America will be visiting. Naomi responds quickly saying "I hope you know they are not coming here in my son's house." "**Listen carefully,** this is my house too and if I want them to come here there is not a damn thing you can do about it. However they are not coming here, they are going to stay at **my house with my family where they will be accepted and comfortable!**" This information is like music to Naomi's ears and much to her relief.

Tamina calls Stella and Mami inviting them out to lunch to share with them the great news of the unexpected visit. "We are having a Welcome home party for them at my parent's home when they arrive from America in two weeks from Wednesday. My aunt and uncle have not been back to Nigeria in more than fifty years and their children will be visiting Nigeria for the first time.

It will be a true Nigerian home coming a very elegant affair! So ladies bring your families all are invited!"

Stella and Mamie in unison declare "That's so nice since our children will be here on vacation at that time." "I would love to meet them. You will also meet Mama, Papa, Cleo and Reggie whom you haven't seen for a long time as well as some other people whom you would remember. I promise, you will have a grand time!" "Girl we are looking forward to."

When Ray spoke to Iyke during one of his many calls to the family Iyke tells him they are going to Nigeria. He requests the phone number where they will be staying so he can call to ensure of their safe arrival. Stealthily Ray gets all the travel plans from Iyke and makes similar arrangements to travel the following day. He soliloquizes briefly "I am going to try once more to get my love back. I was such a fool to let my stupid pride and friends get the best of me. Boy, you never miss the water till the well runs dry, I let the best thing in my life get away. I am going to try my hardest to win her back." He makes sure to locate a Hotel close to Tamina's house to assure that his plans would go off without a hitch.

Tamina re-confirms the travel plans with her Aunt for their arrival into the country and in true fashion of the Sebe-Ankra family they all head to the airport for a special welcome. Since they are expecting five individuals they needed all their cars, Tamina with her brother and sister all drove their respective vehicles.

It is all coming back to them now the last time they were all at this airport as a family was to send Tamina off to America under such sad circumstances. This is in such contrast today, she is here now waiting with her family to welcome her children and the man and woman who became her parents in her new life, a life she believes she would never have had if it wasn't for her parents with her aunt and uncle. The tears begins to flow from her eyes like streams after a wicked storm knowing that her babies will be there with her and still cannot tell them she is truly their mom.

"May I have your attention please, American Airlines flight 4230 from Baltimore Washington International to Murtula Mohammed International has just arrived at Gate 14, came blaring over the Public Address system in the terminal. Tamina's heart sank even more with intrepid anticipation. All she wants to do is to hug her children even if they think they are her cousins and to shower her aunt and uncle with the love and admiration they have been sharing with her since she was fourteen.

Thirty minutes after the announcement Tamina looks up and spots Iyke initially and did a double take only to see Carl and Cindy appear following them her aunt and uncle. With a scream that can only be described as a hawk's cry Tamina took off running towards them and not being able to control her emotions, release a bevy of noises and tears as she reaches out grabbing the twins firstly extremely tight then to her aunt, uncle and cousin. Two minutes later the entire family was able to catch up with the vaulting Tamina after which there is not a dry eye among them.

Two days later Ray arrives. He calls from his cell phone.

"Hi buddy, how are things? I'm just calling to see how you guys are." "Well we got here safely, everybody is ok. Tamina is having a welcome party for us tonight I don't think I'll know anyone there but before the party is over I intend to know all my relatives and then some." "I wish I was there to get to know Tamina's other relatives even though we are not together anymore."

"Y…you had a good thing and you let it get away don't blame anyone but yourself."

"True that…. true that, I have no one else to blame but myself. All I can pray for is another chance at love" he retorted.

"Anyhow I will call you after the party to share the details of what went down."

"Bye tell T hello for me."

Through all this Iyke knowingly neglects to tell Ray that Tamina is re-married.

Chapter XX

The Welcome Party

D-Day is here and the welcome home party is in full swing with a mixed group of people blacks, whites, Nigerians, foreigners and holiday goers along with the special invitees Stella and Mami with their families. Ray walks into the compound and enters the house, it is no alarm for a young white man attending the party as there are many. He gets a drink and walks directly over to Iyke who is in shock,

"What the hell are doing here?"

"I'm here to surprise you. I want to see Nigeria also hope to get my wife back!"

Tamina sees Ray and walks over to him "Ray, what in the world are you doing here?"

"Surprise, Surprise!" giving her a hug.

"I am here with the hope that the one woman whom I love and so badly hurt would give me another chance to be her husband, I want my wife back!"

"Say What? Who is your wife?"

"You woman, I am here to take you home, you will always be my wife!" A voice from behind them said, "I don't think so buddy. This woman is spoken for. **She is my wife she is Mrs. Kelvin Smith!**"

"Is Mrs., who?"

"Yes Ray, I am now Mrs. Kelvin Smith."

Ray stretches out his hand to Kelvin, "I am so sorry buddy I didn't know Tamina remarried."

"Who are you?" Kelvin asks

"Well, I am the ex-husband but my friends and everyone else call me Ray D."

"Ohhh, so you're the famous Mr. O'Donnell. I must thank you for having her return to Nigeria. I owe all my happiness to you. Thanks so much again." As if to rub the dagger even harder into Ray's heart.

Ray gives a grimacing smile and says, "After I heard Iyke and his family were coming to Nigeria I decided to take a trip unknown to them to see if I could win my wife back but I guess … I'm too late; I didn't know she has already remarried. I am soooo sooorry."

"That's ok Ray you see good women don't linger for long, your loss is my gain thanks again buddy!" he retorted with that wicked smile. "You can stay here and have a good time, maybe you'll find another good Nigerian woman but I am going to bet you it wouldn't be T" and with that they all chuckled. Iyke took Ray to his parents who are surprised to see him.

"What are you doing here?" inquires Ruby.

"He is here to see if he could get his wife back!" says Iyke. They all laughed heartily even Ray with some degree of embarrassment.

The party is far more exciting than Tamina and Kelvin could have ever imagined. It's the first time he has had the privilege of meeting more of his in-laws as well as the much touted Stella and Mami. Kelvin is an absolute gentleman throughout the evening as he makes sure everyone is properly taken care of.

Stella and Mami who are special invitees at this affair are so happy to see Tamina's parents, her brother and sister after such a long time and even their spouses and children. They are introduced to Carl and Cindy as Tamina's cousins they then settle in to have a great time a true Nigerian welcome home party until the wee hours of the morning with various sounds of music both traditional and western.

Later the crowd grew with younger people who begin dancing to songs from hip-hop artists as they are shouting "The roof, the roof, the roof is on fire we don't want no water let the mother f...er burn!" as they lift their hands up to show they were ready to raise the roof. Later as the festivities wind down, the tired celebrants and Ray are drifting away slowly, and then the household retires as other families go to their respective homes.

Tamina's weekends are set only for family and to complete household task, the day after the party is Saturday and she's doing no weekend chores instead she's home just laying around munching on bits of food and enjoying the day sitting in the shade of the trees and moving with the shadows.

The phone has been ringing frequently today but none of the calls are hers until Brenda brings her the phone after it rings again, "Auntie it's for you!"

Taking the phone from Brenda she says "Hello!"

"Tamina, I heard you had a welcome home party for your relatives from America and you did not invite me!"

"Who is this? I don't recognize your voice!"

198

"This is Phyllis. Remember me from our final year in Med School?" "Oh yes, Phyllis Danbey. How are you? Where are you?"

"I returned to Nigeria right after graduation and have been here ever since. I work at County General in Lagos and I learnt of the party from my hair stylist Stella. She had to open today for special appointments so she told me while fixing my hair. Tamina I must see you we have a lot to catch up on!"

Tamina is speechless. She never expected to hear from Phyllis after they left Med School she didn't know where she was and what she is doing but is happy to hear from her. "Yes Phyllis I am in Lagos and I've started my own Medical Clinic, tell me how it is we never met at all those medical conferences?" "You must remember those events are set up in two factions doctors in the hospital are done in one session and private practice in another that could be why we never met. Take my number give me a call so we can get together. "Thanks Phyllis I will surely call you, bye!"

Tamina muse; "Phyllis the girl with the motor mouth, she could talk nonstop. It seems as if nothing has changed!" She laughed at the thought. Then reflecting on the register of Licensed Physicians in Nigeria she might have by-passed Phyllis' name since she was not looking for it.

Sometime later Mami calls she's ecstatic and has trouble clearly expressing herself. It took a while for her to calm down and proceed to tell Tamina her view of the party and the great joy it was to have met her husband, parents, sister, brother, nieces, nephews, cousins, aunt and uncle. She had to list them all so as to make her point. The food was exquisite and the drinks just perfect.

"Your wrap Tamina was very fashionable, where did you get it?"

"Oh, I made it. It's my own original design!"

"You should go into the design business also you'll do very well!" They laugh about it and continued with a little banter about Friday's events then they said their goodbyes.

It wasn't too long after that Stella calls. She is cool and deliberate choosing her words carefully so as not to annoy or give the wrong impression. Tamina answers the phone call while sounding tired so Stella makes every effort to wake her up.

"Tamina what happen to you, didn't you have your eye-opener this morning? You sound so flat." They both laughed.

"Stella, you won't believe it, this phone's been ringing all day, it's now two o'clock and I know it is not over as I expect more calls!"

"Tamina, I enjoyed myself at your party last night I met so many people whom I have not seen for a long time. Thanks for inviting my family and I especially since meeting with your family again was a great treat. Your brother has grown to be quite a handsome man, your mom didn't seem to age at all and your father Tamina is still the stalwart he was when we were young, treasure him. Oh, your husband where did you find him? He is totally in love with you. I have not seen such devotion and adoration as he has displayed for you, you're so blessed he's a real keeper. By the way, my son is enquiring about your cousin. Wouldn't it be nice if they can get together?" This causes both of them, to start laughing. They continue to talk of different subjects some current some past while chuckling like when they were just school girls which suggest it was funny or amusing if not both. The time flew by quickly before they both acknowledged it, after which they said their goodbyes promising to talk later. To complete the day's phone exercise, she calls her parents' home to speak to her aunt. "Hello mom, I know you are now just waking up since you went to bed after six this morning. Are the visitors up?" "Yes we all are up since eleven o'clock and we are now watching the BBC-Africa News. Hold on, here is your aunt." Taking the phone Ruby proceeds to talk to her niece, "Hello Tamina, how are you today? Tamina we enjoyed the party so much, thank you. I am so touched to meet so many of the folks with whom I grew up, but sadly a number of them have gone to their ancestors. But after talking with your mother, she up-dated me as best she could of the village. It's exciting. Oh I must go there before I return to America. Am I going to see you later?" "Yes, we'll surely be there." "Well what an end to another lazy Saturday."

Sunday came and both households even Ray went to church. This is the first time all the families and in-laws are able to worship together and it really shows the kind of togetherness they possess. However after church Kelvin goes off to do an errand with his mother and sister while Tamina, Ray, the twins and the rest of the families have lunch at The International Restaurant a local five star eatery where one can order anything on the menu at any time of the day be it breakfast, lunch or dinner. There is also the option of eating any meal from any corner of the earth as international dishes are their highly coveted signature treat. Kelvin, his mother and sister join the party just before the main course is served, since the errand did not take long.

The twins tell Tamina that they are enthralled by the country and they are going to stay in Nigeria and not return to America. Carl says he would like to work alongside her at the clinic to augment the work she is already doing, this makes her extremely happy and she offers him all the support needed to get acquainted.   Cindy says since she is a lawyer like Kelvin she hopes he will get her a position at the Law firm where he is now a senior partner. Finding her a position is no problem since one of their attorneys has accepted a position to the federal bench of the Republic of Nigeria to serve his country so a vacancy does exist. Tamina is elated at the thought of them staying and her inner happiness radiates across her countenance and actions.

Despite the circumstances Kelvin takes Uncle Daan, Ray, Iyke and Carl around the city and near suburbs sight-seeing places of interest and to indigenous restaurants to get a real feel of the culture much to their delight from the point of view of the kitchen. The guys had a great time and Kelvin is extremely happy to know Ray. This tour to Daan serves as a reminder of the old days when he was a young man, feeling the depths of the Nigeria he knew is nostalgic and brings him close to emotional tears, the urge which he has difficulty resisting.

During the next week all members of the families go to the village. So much has changed. Ruby is excited to see the main road which runs through the village is now a broad tarmac covered thoroughfare with street signs, traffic signs and street lights. A number of villagers own cars and motorcycles, there are fewer huts and more substantial buildings and the market place is now an established entity with a large building. The police too now have more than one vehicle and the personnel are well beyond that meager number of so long ago. She is so happy that she insists that they have lunch at the shanty restaurant which still exists with the original dishes, which they all enjoyed immensely. Daan requests that Ruby should have these dishes at their home.

The following day Daan and Ruby go to his village to visit his relatives and observe the changes there. He is not too excited as he learns that most of the people whom he knew are no more and others are gone overseas. The three men with whom he grew up were well advanced in age and could not remember him, despite efforts to refresh their memories. The general population, there is relatively younger and seem a generation or two removed from him. However he did enjoy the time spent there and promised to return at another time.

Uncle Daan, Aunt Ruby, Iyke and Ray return to America after spending one hectic month, feeling satisfied that the time was worth it and all is well. On their way back Ray takes stock of the time spent with Tamina and her family, he is happy but is still grieving at not being able to win her back. Turning to Iyke he shares with him in confidence "It hurts but I'm contented being her friend, I'm going to start dating again and maybe….. Just maybe I will find a woman as good as T or someone close to her standards. Let's face it there isn't another woman out there who can match up with T on any level. I hope we could still be friends." Iyke gives him the pound fist saying "Sure man always!"

A week after his return from Nigeria, Ray moves back into his condo, he calls Katherine inviting her out to dinner to which she gladly accepts. "I know you have been very patient with me but I would like to take things slow, I don't want to make the same mistake again. Are you willing to take the chance with me?"

"Sure, I have been waiting for this call a long time."

They grow closer much to Becky's delight. Some months later they make a forward decision to move in together. This move sends his mother in spirals of gratification as she hugs her husband with surging pleasure.

Chapter XXI

Our New World

It took little time for Cindy and Carl to settle into their new home of Nigeria and into the commune with their family members. Cindy after applying for the position at Stamina Lawyers is immediately accepted and hired. Kelvin who has gained the notoriety and praises from the earlier Ekeh's case, has greater influence in decision making. Cindy given the position of Sr. Associate of International Affairs with direct links to Entertainment Law offices in Beverly Hills, California a position with which she feels comfortable since her major is entertainment law. However it will take some time for her, a waiting period to be able to take the required exams and be admitted to the bar in Nigeria.

Carl begins assisting Tamina at the Clinic with minor surgeries and emergencies as he is awaiting his acceptance from the Nigeria Medical Board. He has help as Tamina asks her old friend Phyllis Danbey to use the weight of her influence to have the application process accelerated. While Carl's record as a doctor in America speaks for itself it's the politics of which they are aware that would delay his acceptance.

There it is The Fortune and Smith Families working side by side, sharing their life and the love of what they do. Tamina more so would sneak away cry and pray thanking the Lord for this blessing "Thank you dear Lord for your mercies ... And for my children to work along with me, they may not know I'm their mother for now but it lifts me up to see them daily!"

They call Kelvin, Uncle K, whom they like very much and he loves them. If they need advice on any matter they go to him. Kelvin reassures them how much he loves Tamina, but his mother and sister are driving them both crazy because we don't have a child.

"Don't they know it's all in God's hands?" Interjects Carl,

"Thank you my son, Thank you, it's in God's hands!" responds Kelvin showing some respect for the young man's vision.

Kelvin's scolding to his mother and Ifoma regarding his wife seems to bring a level of peace to the family especially since they would be sent back to the village should there be a repeat of their unsavory behavior towards Tamina. They didn't want to go back, especially Naomi who, if she returns to the village could not share in her son's wealth.

Yep, peace reigns supreme in the Smith's household.

Chapter XXII

Kelvin's Indisposition

About one year later Kelvin fell ill Tamina takes him to the family doctor who misdiagnoses the complaint. Tamina, though a doctor seeks the expertise of local specialists who could not find his ailment and also make the right diagnosis.

Kelvin's mother and sister are accusing Tamina of bewitching him "She refuses to give him a child now she wants to kill him so she can get all his money, his house and his cars but she is not going to get away with it!" They are so convinced of Tamina's ill-will towards Kelvin, that they make no effort to support her to solve the reason for his illness. His condition worsens and he is admitted to Lagos University Hospital.

Tamina in desperation makes an overseas call to America to her good friend Doctor Ralph Gonzalez with whom she went to medical school. When she told him of Kelvin's condition and how fast he is deteriorating, Ralph decides he would fly to Nigeria to take a look at him. Tamina immediately makes arrangements for Ralph's trip to Lagos. Arriving few days later, Doctor Ralph examines Kelvin and discovers that his kidneys are failing. To survive he needs a transplant as soon as possible, firstly a donor must be found. Immediately the search begins and his name is placed on the national donors' list.

He must remain in hospital awaiting a match. His mother and other family members approach Tamina who is at home preparing to go to the hospital. "You see if you had given him a child he would have had a perfect match. You don't care if he dies so you can get all his money, his house and his cars."

Tamina replies "Why don't you, your daughter and the rest of your family get tested to see if you are a match for him instead of blaming me about a child." Ifoma rebuffs Tamina's statement saying, "We all did but no one's a match."

Kelvin's mother got in Tamina's face saying "You see you see how she is talking back to us, Kelvin is not here to defend you now!" then without any further dialog she slaps Tamina's across the face knocking her to the floor. She gets up rubbing her face in disbelief

"Wait a minute," said Tamina in quiet and deliberate expression "Didn't I warn you never to hit me again you sow?"

Ifoma rushes up to her and pointing a finger in Tamina's face at the same time saying "And what the hell are you going to do? You useless barren heifer! You can't even give my brother a child!"

"Now listen to me carefully, when I married Kelvin I married him only, not you and all his family. When he met me I was and still am a Doctor, have my own business establishment, handling my own money, plus my own house and still do. I don't need Kelvin's money, his house or his cars. Now when it comes to hitting me, that's another issue, I let you get away with it the first time but never again, I don't know how you do it in Nigeria but in America they call it abuse. I swore a long time ago after the pain I went through nobody would ever abuse me again and get away with it, nobody!" Tamina places a back handed slap across Naomi's face and the four other family members then rush to subdue her. Tamina put her martial arts skills to work for her she kicked, slapped and slammed them as they attack her and she gives them a sound trashing, then threw them all out of her house and out of the compound and instructs Kaaren, "You are never to let them in here again!" Kaaren is delighted to do Tamina's bidding since mama had given her such a hard time during the preceding months by having her do tasks outside her job and still expects her to be alert at the gate. She feels some degree of vindication executing the lock-out of mama and the other family members.

Tamina takes a breather, then hops in her Mercedes and heads to the hospital to visit her husband who deeply appreciates her presence. As she greets him with a kiss on his cheek he squeezes her hand and affectionately caresses her face smiling all the while.

"Being the boss really does have its benefits," Tamina keeps saying to herself as she decides to take emergency leave to be with her husband knowing that Carl and the other doctors are capable enough of running the clinic efficiently and effectively.

Knowing what needs to be done for her husband Tamina seeks divine intervention from her God and enlist the services of their chief minister Pastor Ellis Luke, the minister who officiated at their church wedding.

A day after that terrible confrontation at the house with her in-laws Tamina arranges for Pastor Luke to visit Kelvin. Pastor Luke arrives well before Tamina which gives him time to talk with Kelvin unabashedly. She enters his private room while they are talking about his sudden illness and the rapid descent into hospital and now being unable to be the man he once was. Kelvin is sounding depressed and despondent.

"God has a plan my son and we should know everything happens for a reason," Pastor Luke retorts. "I believe that is true Pastor, but why does it have to be this painful?" Kelvin says with a little chuckle.

"He always has a way of getting his point across my son, sometimes it picks us up and sometimes it lands us flat on our backs," as the Pastor tries to comfort Kelvin and giving him hope for better days.

"Well Pastor Luke please tell him I need my husband back right now since there is much work to be done by him, after all I need to have his baby soon." Tamina chimes in as they all start laughing.

Time is of the very essence so every avenue is being explored to find a matching donor. The Local organ donor bank is scrutinized without success and the search even extends internationally to the United Nations Organ Donor Banks without success. The future seems bleak; his demise seems eminent as his condition is further deteriorating. Will a donor be found from some unexpected source in time? Is it possible that his kidneys will repair themselves? What are the possibilities at this ninth hour?

Chapter XXIII

The Revelation

The next day brought with it more prayers and concerns as Kelvin becomes even weaker. His relatives from the village along with Pastor Luke, who come to pray for his recovery and call on his ancestors for their divine help. Amidst the silence the door to his room opens his mother and sisters arrive, Naomi and Ifoma sporting cuts and bruises about their faces the results of the good thrashing delivered at the hands of Tamina. As they move closer to greet Kelvin with a kiss on his forehead the injuries become more evident which creates a perplexing expression on his face but in his weaken state he just gestures his concern. "It's a long story we will talk later," says Ifoma.

In his further weakening state the Pastor begins praying again more fervently and when finished he says the Lord revealed something to him. He requests they all come out into the hall where he surprises them with the revelation to which he's privy.

"There is a way to save him during our communal prayer the Lord spoke to me. Kelvin has a child who could give him a kidney." Pastor Luke exclaimed with utter joy and merriment.

"A child!" someone in the group questions aloud,

"What the hell are you talking about?" Tamina yells abruptly "Pastor I don't mean to swear but where in God's name did Kelvin get this child?"

"The Lord showed me when Kelvin was a young man, a mere teenager he did wrong to a young woman, and he must go to your village that he haunted with vicious crimes in his youth. He must do three things urgently." using his fingers to gesture his number of points he continues. "One, he must find that family, two… make genuine peace with them and three find out where the child is who can help him. This is the sole hope to save his life."

"But Pastor how could he go when he is lying here dying?" "Then **you…. His closest blood relatives must** go!"

Chioma turns to her mother and demandingly asks "What is the Pastor talking about? What did Kelvin do and where are we going to find this family and convince them after all their pain to help us save his life?"

"My child I don't know what the Pastor is talking about, but let's go to the village and see what we can find out, I don't know where to start maybe we can find the Elders to help us. Tamina you don't have to come with us stay here with your husband we'll find that family to help save your husband, my son!" "And my brother" said Chioma, "Whom I love so much!" Promptly they took off hopefully to find this mystery family.

They arrive in the village of Ngoziville at dusk knowing that every minute counts so they immediately seek an audience with the Elders. Normally at dusk it is known that all elders congregate under the large tree in the center of the village where they discuss current events and address concerns of villagers who are peeved or have other issues which need to be settled, but it is also a known fact their sole intent for being there is the pure consumption of the free palm wine given to them by the village people and the possibility of copulating with some the many young girls in the square who flaunt themselves most alluringly.

Presenting them with palm wine and a small gift Naomi explains to them her reason for returning to her old village and the urgency of finding this family.

"Oh great elders of our community my reason for coming to our ancestors village is to seek help for my son Kelvin. I know you remember my family and the trouble my son used to create as a child, today he lies helpless in a hospital bed in Lagos. During a prayer session with his pastor a revelation came to him. He said my son as a teenager hurt someone in Ngoziville and he needs to make it right. My husbands, I know you wouldn't know all the people he might have hurt with his thuggery but we don't know where to start looking."

An Elder after listening to her plight remarks to them "Akan and Ameka were his closest friends but they no longer live in the village however their families are still here. They live at the farther east end of the village pass the mechanic shop ask there for Eloise, Akan's mother and Charlotte who's Ameka's mother." Expressing their gratefulness to them all, Naomi and her family head quickly in the direction given.

The reunion of the families is short with small pleasantries as the urgency so evident in the manner of their questions. They would visit both families who tell them Ameka is in Abuja and Akan is in Lagos and giving Naomi several cards bearing both their telephone numbers, home and business addresses.

Within minutes after leaving the families they were back on the highway heading to Akan knowing with every second past Kelvin is dying, Chioma starts to pray for guidance "Please God please let us find Akan and hope he knows what the Pastor is talking about!" With a trek of over five hours ahead of them they knew they will not get to Akan until 8 am, it worries them all but held steadfast that Akan will have the answers they seek to save Kelvin's life.

They found Akan, he's an executive for a large multinational firm in Lagos, and he recognizes Kelvin's Mother and showers her with hugs and kisses while giving her compliments as he enquires of them,

"What may I do for you?" She tells him she lives in the City of Lagos too, he responded,

"How is Kelvin, is he still in America?"

"No, he is back in Nigeria as a lawyer at a Lagos legal firm **Stamina Lawyers**." "That was Kelvin, my friend Kelvin? I didn't connect the dots!" "Yea, that was your friend Kelvin, but I need your help badly!"

"Mama anything just ask. Kelvin was my best friend along with Ameka. Ameka and I keep in touch the only one we haven't spoken to in a long time is Kelvin."

"Well if you don't help me you may never get the chance to speak to him again."

"What do you mean Mama you are scaring me?"

"Kelvin is lying near death in Lagos University Hospital."

Chioma speaking slowly and intently

"Akan I want you to think back to when you were young men. Please tell me the truth you are not going to get into any trouble you will be saving Kelvin's life. When you were young did Kelvin do something horrible to a young woman that you can remember?" Akan turns his face away. Chioma grabs him by the arm

"Please, Kelvin is dying and we have to find the family of that young woman to save his life."

"Auntie, please remember we were boys, wicked boys. Frivolous, we did not realize the wrong that we were doing. We weren't caught for that crime but we got caught for other things and went to prison for a short time. Prison was the wake-up call for us after which we vowed never to go to jail again. We went our separate ways to make something of our lives that's when Kelvin left for America, Ameka went to Abuja and I came here to Lagos."

"Akan we know all that, now tell us what did you do and what is the name of the girl and her family?"

"One day three young girls were coming from the river fetching water we ambushed them, two of the girls got away but we got one and raped her all three of us. She couldn't see our faces, as we wore masks."

225

"God forbid!" snapping her fingers, Chioma exclaimed "What is the name of that family?"

"I think the name was Sebe-Ankra. I heard they live in a Lagos suburb now. Somebody came from America and moved them from the village to Lagos."

"Ok Mama we have to find these Sebe-Ankra people fast!" said Chioma.

"Mama let me make a call to Ameka he must know that Kelvin is gravely ill and needs our help. I will tell him to meet us at Lagos University Hospital and I will go with you now."

They all headed to the hospital there they meet Stella, Mami, Tamina and Pastor Luke. They told Tamina of their findings. "You said what? Sebe-Ankra? That is my family name!" shouts Tamina hysterically.

Chioma spoke, "Do you know the woman they are talking about?" Just then Pastor Luke interrupts them saying,

"Wait, wait the Lord just revealed something more to me. There are two children a boy and a girl, twins!"

Tamina is overwhelmed, she runs out of the Hospital gets into her car and drives to her Mother's house, going through some intersections without even stopping at the red lights or stop signs, crying and soliloquizing, "God you mean of all the men in the world, I had to fall in love and marry Kelvin one of the men who raped me when I was thirteen years old. God how can you be so cruel? Now that I know it's him I feel every time we made love he was raping me all over again. God what do I do?" Tamina gets into the house crying not realizing everyone who was at the hospital has followed her leaving Kelvin to solitude in his room.

In Cynthia's arms she breaks down, her understanding mother comforts her, holding Tamina to her breasts inquires "What is going on, why you crying my baby?"

"Mama, where are Carl and Cindy?"

"They are not home. What happen?" she ask more concerned. Still crying, "Dad do you know my husband Kelvin?"

"Yes, what happen, did you find him a donor or is he dead?"

"Mom and Dad Kelvin my husband is one of the guys who raped me when I was thirteen years old!"

"What, didn't you know? Did he know?" I don't think so but dad that's not all; Carl and Cindy are his children!"

Chioma and Kelvin's mother both in utter surprise speak simultaneously "But I thought they are your cousins!"

"No! They are my children, they don't know. How in the world am I going to tell them that I am their mother and the man they know as Uncle K is their father who raped me when I was thirteen years old and now one of them has to give him a kidney to save his life?"

Stella and Mami are astonishingly surprised they shouted out together "Those guys raped you that day and you married one of them!" Then Stella lamented "You mean to tell me that out of that rape you have two children? Those things only happen in fairy tales and now those children have to come back to save his life?"

Pastor Luke answered, "Ladies! Ladies, she did not know it was him but that is not the issue here, then putting his arm around Tamina "Sister Tamina, do you remember when you returned from America you came to my office and told me about what happened all those years ago, I asked you if you ever see them again what will you do, do you remember what you said?"

"Yes Pastor I remember, I don't know what they look like but I have forgiven them a long time ago. Pastor could you imagine in your wildest dreams, in a world of so many men, the culprit would turn out to be my husband Kelvin a very loving and caring man?"

"Sister Tamina I know but those children are his and one of them could save his life."

"Yes Pastor, he's their father." she said in most resignedly lowering her head and proceeding to dry her eyes which are overflowing the napkin, it seems that the more she dries, the more tears flow.

Chapter XXIV

The Gift of Love

Kelvin's mother and sister Ifoma kneel down before Tamina emotionally grabbing her around the knees and thighs making tearful appeals, "Please, please my daughter help him, talk to the children. We are sorry for all the wrong things we have done to you we never knew what you went through. Will you ever forgive us?"

"I have forgiven you even while you were hurting me; but it's their decision to make."

During this debacle Carl and Cindy walk in and utter "Whose decision Sister Tamina, what's going on, why are these people here on their knees crying?"

Tamina speaks "Carl and Cindy I have something to tell you." Carl casually responded "What? That you are our mother!"

"What? You knew!"

Cindy is happy and they respond spontaneously "Yes, Auntie Ruby and Uncle Daan told us on our twenty first birthday but they ask us not to mention it to you. This is one of the reasons we decided to come to Nigeria hoping and praying for the day when we can rightfully call you mummy!" They hug and kiss her as the tears ran down their cheeks. "Don't cry mummy, it's all good now we know who we are!" They are sounding joyful but couldn't contain their tears which is now soaking Carl's shirt, but it didn't matter. Everybody is crying and somehow enjoying it.

Chioma speaks "Since that secret is out what are we going to do about the other secret, shall I tell them?"

"No!" said Tamina's father "I'll tell them!" he has them sit down and tells them the whole story.

"So you see you are with your own people now you know the lines to your ancestors of your mother and your father. We are your grand-parents, your mother's parents." Hugging his wife, "Since you know everything, it's up to the two of you to decide if you want to help him, that man your father!" Without any hesitation and a new sense of urgency Carl and Cindy spoke in agreement "Let's go to the hospital to see Uncle K. Does he know about all of this?"

"No, we did not get a chance to tell him," answers Tamina.

"Ok then we'll do it together. When we came to Nigeria he treated us so well we got to love him like a father, never knowing he really is!" Cindy emotionally speaking, "now just picture coming to Nigeria not only gave us our mother but also our father and all the ancestors. Oh, thank you God almighty for making this possible!" Pastor Luke said, "Amen and Amen, in Jesus name Amen! You are so brave and kind." Then he lays his hands on the twins blessing them. They are happy, excited and nervous as a bag of emotions all at the same time but are in reserved silence as they travel back to the hospital. Their inner joy and their sudden new merriment are like a pleasurably sharp pain which isn't going away and they didn't want it to wane. They just want to hold on to it.

They are both tested of course both a perfect match but Carl decides he wants to be the one donating the gift of life to uncle K and he did with the surgery ending in great success. Kelvin is spared from death.

Several days later Kelvin is fit and ready to leave the hospital, Carl is released three days prior. The families gathered at the Smith's residence to welcome Kelvin home and toast to his good health. They all sat around telling Kelvin of the happenings. Akan and Ameka get down on their knees begging forgiveness of the entire family while Kelvin laid on the sofa, crying and pleading for his wife's forgiveness.

This is the first time after more than thirty-two years that Tamina is really able to see the men who violated her. For the first time she stood face to face with her fate the men who changed her life forever how cruel it might have been or was it?

The deluge of tears comes back again this time it is with deep mixed emotions which couldn't have been expressed in any other way. The other family members and in-laws all share the emotion in a very special manner, each being touched and touching others accordingly.

Repeatedly Akan and Ameka constantly beg her for forgiveness. When she looks at them upon their knees and in their eyes remorse, they seem so pitiful. Tamina is moved with compassion and forgives all over again. She goes over to her husband and embraces him feeling certain compassion and love for him which she has never felt before all she could say at this time is, "I love you all!" With love Carl and Cindy joining them solemnly express the same sentiment.

At this point Tamina calmly announces "There is one more thing I would like to say, I have been offered the position of Minister of Health and

Social Services by the President of Nigeria and he has invited me to meet with him at the Presidential Palace in two weeks. I would like to know your opinion of this development." After some silence someone asks, "What will become of the Clinic if you take that job?" "Well, Dr. Jeffery Walker who is the senior doctor along with Carl and the other doctors will run the clinic. But I haven't made up my mind as yet. After my visit with the President I'll decide, Cindy I would like you to accompany me there." "Sure mom, it feels so good calling you mom!" There is a roar of approving laughter which fills the room. Kelvin winces with mild pain as he moves his body with excitement of the news.

Kelvin's mother is overjoyed and is gloating over the fact she is indeed twice a grand-mother by Kelvin. Naomi has suddenly developed a beam and a broader smile than she ever had. When she sees the children hug their parents, she couldn't resist the urge to express her love and adoration for them all. She embraces Tamina with true remorse begging her forgiveness. Ifoma feels left out and joins her mother.

The children then approach and embrace their grandmother and cry for joy to know they have now found their paternal lineage. Chioma joins them and together with their father propped up on the sofa they now know who they are and have no doubt about it. Kelvin seizes the opportunity to hold on to Carl and Cindy's hands, "Please forgive us for what we did to your mother all those years ago. We were just wicked, irresponsible young men who did not realize the harm we were doing to peoples' lives." Akan and Ameka join in the group saying "We are so sorry, please forgive us." Cindy replies, "If my mother can find it in her heart to forgive you, who are we not to do the same. You are forgiven. May God bless you bountifully! Now Uncle K, when Carl and I came to this country the way you took us under your wings, you treated us like a father to his children not realizing you are. We watch you with our mother, your loving kindness and attentiveness to her. Why wouldn't we forgive you? If we didn't, Carl would not have given you a kidney. So let's forget the past and bury it there. Let's move on to a brighter future. Now what should we call you Uncle K or Dad?" Everyone laughed. Kelvin replies, "Call me anything, but please don't ever stop calling me. I love you all. Thank you!"

During the ensuing months Kelvin returns to full health and is back to his office. Tamina calls Aunt Ruby telling her of the situation with Kelvin and his recovery with Carl's participation, then the biggest news that Kelvin is the children's father. To which Aunt Ruby and Uncle Daan burst into a joyful prayer. Just then Iyke enters the room, hears the news and is overwhelmed with joy for Tamina and the twins, he could only say "May God bless and keep them together." During this conversation Ruby tells Tamina a bit of exciting news, "Your uncle has finally retired. We are considering touring the world, taking trips everywhere our hearts desire. So being in Nigeria is a definite option." "Well, it's about time. Uncle Daan has worked all his adult life."

After conferencing with the President, Tamina accepts the position as Minister of Health and Social

Security, leaving her private practice to the capable hands of the venerable doctors and staff at the Center.

There are troubling issues in every family, the Smith family is not immune to such circumstances but manage to successfully navigate around them with minimum disruptions. They're now facing the potentially damning situation as the violators of several decades ago are identified and much negative reaction by Kelvin is seen. He rejects cohabiting with his family and from time to time he is withdrawn, retreating into the realm of alcoholism, though not ever admitting to the condition. He couldn't come to terms with the fact that Tamina has forgiven him and his friends for their savagery of her that far back. He feels inadequate and less than his regular self, yep he feels less than a man.

Weeks passed and Kelvin's alcoholism grew more profound, it is time for an intervention. Tamina, the two children and a friend sat down with Kelvin to bring him back to his family and further prevent him from harming himself.

Sitting in a circle around Kelvin Tamina begins,

"Kelvin my love, for weeks we have watched as you descend into an abyss fueled by alcohol. You increasingly return home later and later every night as if you are trying to avoid me. Begging you to share what is wrong with you only to be met with silence."

"Enough!!! I work hard every day to give you the lifestyle that you so rightly deserve and you stand here accusing me of being a bad husband," Kelvin quickly whipped.

"NOW LISTEN Kelvin and LISTEN good, I want you to realize the problem before it came to this but instead it just got worst. You refuse to talk so I will……., YOU NEED TO GET YOUR ACT TOGETHER NOW, I AM SICK AND TIRED OF YOUR ABSENCE IN THIS FAMILY, I am sick of your LIES of nothing being wrong and I am totally fed up with your pity party with yourself. What is it, is it my new governmental position, or is it my paycheck being bigger than yours. What the hell is it???? Tamina declares with such utter frustration.

The tears began to flow down her face and of his daughter; it then becomes clear, that he has hurt the most important people in his world. "My God … all I want to do is to find a way to get beyond the pain of my actions to my Tamina and my kids," Kelvin said with open remorse, "What have I done?!!!"

A huge silence descends on the group, the stranger in the room stands in front of Kelvin.

"Mr. Smith my name is Jake Roberts I am a friend of Cindy's, we attended college back in the United States I am a therapist working at Lagos General Hospital. I was observing this interaction as Cindy shared with me the strange behavior you have displayed as of late. Sir you have so much pain within you, you have approached this sit down totally on the defensive, your words display fear and unworthiness to be happy in your life."

Kelvin looks up, "Mr. Roberts, forgive me but our family business is our family business so butt out."

Cindy jumps up and shouts. "Stop it!! Dad you're scaring me, listen to Jake he wants to help, please……."

Carl chimes in "Yeah, Just try, I cannot handle losing you after so many years of not knowing you."

"Alright, alright I will" Kelvin finally relents.

"As a boy I was misguided and dumb, my friends and I raped this wonderful woman who is now my wife with Cindy and Carl being the fruits of my crime. I didn't know Cindy's mother was the girl I raped and the woman I would marry. The worst part was the kids who were products of this rape were the ones who saved my life and to top it all off this angelic woman … my wife simply forgive me and my friends just like that. I did so much wrong to these people and I received no punishment. I do not deserve her or anyone of my kids. I should have died but they saved my life."

"Mr. Smith it is o.k. to forgive yourself, your family has done so" Jake shared.

"Dad we love you, you were young, wicked and dumb back then, today you are not that person anymore."

With tears still flowing down her cheeks Tamina speaks up "Honey, I was angry for a long time as a young girl I blamed the world but as I grew older I learnt to forgive and love. My life has been truly blessed; I was surrounded by so many people who wanted nothing but the best for me. I found my purpose in life."

"Mr. Smith with time you will learn to forgive yourself as your family has already done, you are a strong man with so many people depending on you to be the family leader, it may be hard now but in time all will be right. Should you need to talk I will always find the time, I know what you mean to your family so I would endeavor to go above and beyond to help as much as possible."

Kelvin stands up and thanks Jake for his time and kind words followed up with a simple question, "Jake I see you are not married …. Should I think you are interested in making my daughter your wife," with a roar of laughter everyone made sure to add their bit. Jake then replies "I see you're feeling well already" The laughter continues much to Kelvin's relief.

Chapter XXV

Then & Now

It was the regular weekly family dinner at Tamina's parent's estate something everyone looks forward to, the preparation and cooking was now in the hands of Tamina who is being groomed to be the family's matriarch as mom and dad enter their golden years. As time passed Tamina's parents would sit under the mango tree in the compound in their favorite love seat swing to enjoy the cool breeze while drinking lemonade and old talk. On one such occasion he mentions the richness of the love which Kelvin and Tamina share with the children and their attentiveness towards them.

"Cynthia my dear, we worked hard in our time but we are blessed to have our two beautiful daughters and a son, and now two sons-in-law and a daughter-in-law and all our grandchildren. They are really blessed. I know that I will be resting in peace when I go to join my ancestors." "Don't worry my husband. Everything will be alright. The ancestors are pleased and already protecting them! Don't you see how Kelvin has changed to be more successful, rich and respected?" He readily agrees. Then taking up his glass, drinks his lemonade slowly savoring each mouthful, while caressing his wife's shoulder and between sips he caresses her like old times and they kiss smiling at each other. That smile in younger years was suggestive to the next step where they would vacate the swing to go upstairs. Now they savor the memory of those days and just quietly hugging and holding on to each other contented as they slowly swing.

✳ ✳ ✳ ✳ ✳

Notes

A great epilogue of a woman who was once a victim and now has evolved into a VICTOR.

June Griffith

TO

JOHN FOLKES

Thanks for your design and layout

of the book cover

ROY JEFFERY ROSS

To the memory of a person whom I proudly called one of my sons during the preparation of this book a special dedication to him who passed on January 5, 2015, before publication.

The Family misses him very much.

May his soul

REST IN PEACE!